S0-BZO-376

THE HEARTH & EAGLE

This is a vivid and colourful tale, showing the growth of a New England town with its change of industries, against the wider historical background of the American continent.

Miss Seton gives life and colour to a long gallery of portraits. Her story has a vigour and a gusto which sweeps the reader eagerly along.

Also by the same author

Dragonwyck
My Theodosia
The Turquoise
Foxfire
Katherine
The Winthrop Woman
Devil Water
Avalon
The Mistletoe and Sword

...d available in Coronet Books

The Hearth & Eagle

Anya Seton

CORONET BOOKS
Hodder Paperbacks Ltd., London

First published November 1948
Fourth impression 1961
This edition (reset) 1964
Second impression 1966
Third impression 1967
Fourth impression 1968
Fifth impression 1969
Sixth impression 1971

---

*The characters and situations in this book are
entirely imaginary and bear no relation to any real
person or actual happening.*

This book is sold subject to the condition that
it shall not, by way of trade or otherwise, be
lent, re-sold, hired out or otherwise circulated
without the publisher's prior consent in any
form of binding or cover other than that in
which this is published and without a similar
condition including this condition being
imposed on the subsequent purchaser.

Printed and bound in Great Britain for
Coronet Books,
Hodder Paperbacks Ltd,
St. Paul's House, Warwick Lane,
London, E.C.4
by Hazell Watson & Viney Ltd,
Aylesbury, Bucks

ISBN 0 340 15699 6

AUTHOR'S NOTE

MARBLEHEAD, Massachusetts, the background to this story, is typical of many New-England sea-coast towns, in the development and decline of two out of three of the industries which have supported it through the years, and at first I had no intention of naming it specifically. But as I began research over two years ago, I soon discovered that Marblehead is far too vivid, charming and fiercely individualistic to be flattened into a type. As I returned there again and again and studied the material more deeply, the town itself produced the story of Hesper and her family and the old inn. I have tried to be accurate in presenting every event which affected actual town history. There is a wealth of fine material, and I am extremely grateful to all the Marbleheaders, old-timers and (comparative) new-comers, who have generously given me of their help and interest. I also want to thank the staff members at the Essex Institute in Salem, the Abbot Hall library and the Historical Society in Marblehead for their co-operation.

There are many published works treating of the town, but for the period I was trying to cover, the most valuable were Samuel Roads's *History and Traditions of Marblehead* and Joseph S. Robinson's *The Story of Marblehead*; and of course the files of the *Marblehead Messenger*, and other contemporary newspapers.

For the early part of the story I studied dozens of fascinating source books, but I am particularly indebted to Sidney Perley's and Duncan Phillips's histories of Salem, and above all to Governor Winthrop's own carefully detailed Journal, in which I was able to follow the day-by-day incidents of that historic voyage.

The Honeywood family and all the main characters are fictitious, though I have made use of some of Marblehead's typical names.

A. S.

CHAPTER ONE

ON the night of the great storm, the taproom was deserted. Earlier, men had wandered in for beers or rum-flip—shoremen all of them now, too old to go out with the fishing fleet. They had drunk uneasily, the pewter mugs shaking in their vein-corded hands, while they listened to the rising wind. Ever more boisterous gusts puffed down the big chimney, scattering fine ash over the scrubbed boards. In the great harbour, two hundred yards away, the mounting breakers roared up the shingle, muffling the clink of mugs on the table and the men's sparse comments.

Hesper, crouching on her stool in the kitchen hearth, could see into the taproom through the half-open door. She watched her mother's face. Ma stood stiffly behind the counter at the far end of the taproom, and she was listening to the storm, too. Even while she made change for the beer drinkers or turned the spigot over a mug, her eyes would slide away to the windows and her big freckled face grow glum and watchful.

This seemed queer to Hesper, because she herself loved the storm. She luxuriated in the delicious feeling it gave her, because it was safe and warm in here. The kitchen and the whole house closed around and held her safe, the way Gran did sometimes when she was feeling good. Outside, the storm was roaring and stamping like Reed's bull roared and stamped in the pasture over on the Neck, but the bull couldn't get at you, nor could the storm. The house was stronger.

Hesper pulled her stool outside of the fireplace and leaned her head against the panelled oak cupboard where Ma kept the spare pots and skillets.

The kitchen smells lulled her. The molasses and pork smell from the bean-pots in the brick oven, the halibut stew bubbling softly on the trivet near the blazing pine logs, the smell of beeswax that had been rubbed into the long oak table and the benches, and the hard pine settle that was dreadful old fashioned, Ma said. The settle had been right there by the fireplace near two hundred years, an eyesore Ma said, all scarred like that from jack-knives and pitted with spark burns. But Pa wouldn't get rid of it. He liked the old things that had always been here.

Another crash hurled itself on the house, and a new sound mixed in it. A slapping wetness. The window-panes ran with water.

"Rain's come," said old Simon Grubb, wiping his mouth on the back of his hand. "Dor-r-ty weather making. Don't like 'em from sou'west. Means they start in the Carib. This is goin' to be worser'n regular September line stor-rm." He heaved himself up from the table, slid three pennies on the counter by Ma's arm. She picked them up and dropped them in the tin cash-box.

"Think it'll travel up to the Banks?" she said. Her voice was just the way it always was, quick and rough, but a quiver ran through Hesper.

The fear in her mother slid across the taproom, through the door into the bright kitchen. Now she saw fear in all of them, in the three silent old men who did not answer her mother's question but filed out of the door, their steps slow and careful, feeling the floor as if they were pacing a heaving, slippery deck. While the door was open to let the shoremen out, the storm blew into the house with the boom of the waves just across Front Street.

"Ma," whispered Hesper, "I'm scared." She ran to her mother, burying her face in the brown calico skirts. "Maybe the sea'll get at us—don't let it get at us."

Susan Honeywood shoved the heavy iron bolt across the door. "It might," she said indifferently. "But the house'll stand." She gave the child a brisk shove. "Get the mop. Floor's all wet. Nothing'll happen to us."

"But you was scared, Ma," persisted the child, though already her panic had passed, the house closed around again, comforting and protecting.

Susan wiped the beer rings from the table in the taproom, shut that door too, and stirred the halibut stew before speaking. Her words when they came seemed to spring from an angry compulsion. "Have you so soon forgot Tom and Will?" she snapped over her shoulder to the puzzled child.

Hesper stared up at her mother's face, hurt by the sudden hostility, and yet she had always known Ma loved the boys better.

"But they're away off on the Banks with the fleet," she whispered.

Susan slapped the pewter plates on to the table. "And so will this storm be—tomorrow or next. It's like the one in twenty, afore I met your Pa." Her full lips folded themselves into a pale line. She untied the apron from around her stout waist. "Call your Pa—supper's on. I'll go in and see if your Gran's got enough wit for eating tonight."

Hesper swallowed, listening to her mother's heavy tread entering the kitchen bedroom. Ma didn't like Pa's old granny, but she didn't usually sound so angry when she spoke of her—most times when Gran acted queer, Ma'd be kind enough, feeding her from the silver porringer with the special spoon Gran always used, even rocking her in the long cradle when Gran got one of those fits when she'd cry and cry and think she was a baby again. Hesper loved Gran, loved her stories and her warm comforting arms on the good days, and accepted the bad days without wonder.

Hesper walked across the kitchen and knocked on her father's door. He spent the greater part of his life in that little lean-to room that had been built for a loom-room years before even Gran had come to the house. Only now it was just called "Pa's room." It had a desk and a Franklin stove, and so many books piled on the floor and up the walls that there was hardly any place to stand.

Pa opened the door at once—sometimes he didn't—and smiled down at the child. His near-sighted eyes puckered around the corners, and his stooping shoulders seemed too frail to hold up the long thin body.

"It's a wild night, Hesper," he said dreamily, lingering over her name. From the moment of her birth in an April twilight he had loved this child as he loved no one else, and he had over-ridden his wife's impatient objections and named the baby Hesper, after the evening star.

He touched the child's red curls with his bony ink-stained fingers and, shambling after her into the kitchen, sat down at the table.

Hesper filled his plate with the steaming halibut stew which he pushed away absently, still held in the dreams that enriched his solitary hours. He repeated slowly:

> "Rough wind, that moanest loud
> Grief too sad for song;
> Wild wind, when sullen cloud
> Knells all the night long. . . ."

Hesper was used to his quotations, and usually she liked the sound of them and the enchanted pictures they made in her mind; but tonight she felt kinship with her mother, who entered the kitchen to hear the last lines.

"God-blost it, Roger," she cried, "I'll not stand for that quiddling poetizing tonight. What do you know of grief, or knells, or aught else, for ever shut up in your room with them books?" She shoved his plate back in front of him, and banged the coffee-pot down on the table.

Roger Honeywood lifted his head and looked at her. "I merely thought, Susan, that Shelley had rather well expressed the mood of the night." His tone strove to be sarcastic and to show a gentlemanly reproof, though his hands trembled and he looked towards the child for the eager response she usually gave him. But Hesper was staring at her mother, who made a strange rough sound in her throat. "To hell I pitch your Shelley, whoever the bostard may be. D'you hear that storm out younder? D'you have wit enough to know what it may mean, you buffleheaded loon?"

Her shrewd green eyes were blazing, her freckled face suffused with dull red.

Hesper saw her father retreat, seeming to shrivel into himself, but he said, "Spoken like a true Marblehead fishwife."

Again Susan made the sound in her throat. "'Tis what I am. I come from fisher folk, and so do you for all you never set foot in a dory near thirty year—for you weren't no good as a fisherman—nor no good at being a tavern keeper, neither; nor at being a fine gentleman at the college."

Hesper saw the colour leave her father's face, and she hoped for anger to replace it—anger to match her mother's. Why couldn't he shout too —hit out, even strike at that flushed, furious face across the table?

But there was silence in the kitchen except for the woman's heavy breathing. Then, outside, another gust threw itself against the house and a branch crashed off the big chestnut tree.

Susan's hands unclenched, she lowered her head. "Don't mind me, Roger," she said dully. "Eat your supper. I'm grouty tonight with the storm." She walked to the fire and poked the smouldering logs. "But they be your sons, too," she added very low.

It seemed that Roger had not heard. He sat staring at his plate, his thin hand turning and twisting the tin fork. Around and past the child there flowed an emotion which she dimly felt. There had been anger, as there often was, and now it was gone, replaced in her mother by an unexpected appeal—that carried with it the hopelessness of true answer.

But Roger did answer after a minute. "I see no cause for worry about the boys. The fleet's weathered many a storm, if this should reach to the Grand Banks, which I doubt."

Susan carried her plate and Hesper's to the wooden sink across the room. "I saw old Dimond on the Burying Hill last night," she said. "He was waving his arms and beating about the gravestones, pointing towards the Banks."

Hesper felt a thrill of awe. All the children knew about Old Dimond, the wizard, and his queer daughter, Moll Pitcher, who lived long ago.

"Nonsense," said Roger, standing up. "There aren't any ghosts. It's not like you to be fanciful, Susan."

His wife pumped water into the sink, and the pewter plates rattled against the spout. "He came to warn when our men're in danger, same as he always did. You know naught about it. You're a landsman."

"I'm a Marbleheader, the same as you. Eight generations of Honeywoods have lived in this house. Don't forget that, Susan."

The woman's massive shoulders twitched. "I'm not like to," she snapped, "with you dinging at it day in day out."

The child stared anxiously from one to the other. Now Ma was getting angry again. Not on account of the Honeywoods exactly; Ma was a Dolliber, and her family had been here as long as any, but it was because Pa . . .

Hesper went to her mother and tugged at her skirt. "I wish the boys *was* here at home, Ma," she said earnestly, trying to fill the need and forestall the renewed attack.

Susan frowned. "Well, it wouldn't be fitting if they was. Men must go far to work and fight—and the women must bear it. Most men," she added, looking at Roger.

The child's hand dropped. Her impulse had done no good. Pa's face had its cold, shut look. He walked back to his room, and the books and the pages and pages of writing that he never talked to people about. They heard the bolt slide in the door.

Susan trod around the kitchen, placing the pewter dishes behind their racks in the old built-in dresser, adding water to the bean-pot in the brick oven, scattering the embers in the great fireplace.

"Go to bed," she said to Hesper, who had long been expecting this command, and could measure by its tardiness the extent of her mother's preoccupation. She obediently picked up the candle her mother had lighted. It flickered wildly in the draughts that blew down the chimney and from under the door.

"Here, give it me. You'll burn the house down." The big middle-aged woman and the small red-haired girl mounted the stairs. Susan waited until the child stood in her long cotton nightgown.

"Say your prayers."

The child knelt by her cot. "Now I lay me down to sleep . . ." And at the end she added timidly, "Please, dear God, keep Tom and Willy safe." And looked up to her mother for approval.

By the guttering light she saw the grim face above her soften. "Amen," said the woman, and Hesper crept into bed, comforted. Her mother bent over with a rare caress, and as she did so they heard a muffled thud below, and the house trembled a little.

"What is it, Ma?" cried the child, struggling up again. Susan went to the window and pressed her face against the small panes.

"It's the sea," she said. "The water's over the Front." Hesper crowded to the window beside her mother; together they watched the heaving blackness outside. There was no lane, nor yard; the thin film of shiny blackness lapped up to the great chestnut tree before the house, showing the jagged points of rocks pushed up from the cove. "Ma, what'll it do?" whispered Hesper. The woman lifted the child and put her into bed.

"The house'll stand," she said. "Go to sleep." And Hesper knew instant security. Ma was always right. Ma was strong. Strong as the house that had been here so long. Gran was strong too—even when she cried and wanted to be rocked. You felt it wasn't really her, it was as if she was making believe. And Pa—he wasn't strong, but he had Ma and Gran and the house—and me too, she thought.

All night the storm blew, and sometimes waves swirled around the rock foundation of the house and poured into the cellar, but Hesper slept.

It was three weeks before they got the news, and for Hesper the night of the storm was only a shadowy memory. Driftwood had been gathered, rocks rolled off the road, and seaweed thrown back to sea. The small craft which had been blown high on shore and on the causeway to the Neck had been salvaged. At the Honeywood home no sign of the storm remained, except the scar on the big chestnut tree where the limb blew off.

The news came to the Honeywoods first. A boy flew into the taproom crying that a schooner had been sighted off Halfway Rock. Zeke Darling, the lighthouse keeper, had sent word it looked like John Chadwick's *Hero*.

Susan shut the taproom, threw a shawl over her shoulders, and ran to the nearest high ground, on the ramparts of ruined Fort Sewall. She paid no attention to Hesper, who trotted after her, much interested. All over town people were hurrying to vantage points, up to the lookout on the Burial Hill, and crowding up the steeple on the Old North. Silently the women and children watched the schooner round the point of the Neck and glide into the Great Harbour. Some of the children started to cheer, greeting the vanguard of the overdue fleet in the traditional manner. But there was no answering cheer from the men on board. The tiny figures on the deck seemed to move about in a listless and mechanical way.

Susan made a sound under her breath and began to walk down the path. Hesper looked up at her curiously, but did not dare speak. They threaded their way around the fish-flakes at Fort Beach, and up Front Street past home, and then Lovis Cove and Goodwin's Head, and at each step others joined them, silent, shawled women like Susan, excited children held in check by the tension of their elders. They reached Appleton's Wharf as the *Hero* made fast. No one spoke, and Captain Chadwick walked solemnly down the plank, the plod of his heavy sea-boots thumping like hammer strokes in the stillness.

"It's bad," he said, shaking his head and not looking at anyone; "tor-rible bad." Above his beard his face was grey-white as a cod's belly.

The crowd stayed silent another minute, then Susan pressed forward into the empty space near the captain.

"How many lost?" she asked quietly, as she had been quiet since the night of the storm.

The skipper pulled off his sou'wester. "Eleven vessels I know of, ma'am. All hands."

"The *Liberty*?"

He bowed his head. "I saw her go down not half a mile away. We could do nothing. Our own mains'l went like a tor-rn pocket handker-chief."

Susan stepped back, and others filled her place. The air grew harsh with despairing questions. The *Sabine*, the *Pacific*, the *Trio*, the *Warrior* —the agonizing list grew. Sixty-five men and boys had been lost. Scarce a home in Marblehead that had no kin amongst the drowned, and from the crowd behind a woman's voice raised in a long moaning wail.

Susan turned and pushed her way back through the people. Hesper followed close. She was awed and excited. Ma had been right. The great storm had got the fishing fleet—and Tom and Willy. She felt no special sorrow. Her brothers had been big men of sixteen and eighteen, away fishing half the year, and with no time for her when they were home. Cousin Tom Dolliber'd been on the *Liberty*, too. So he was gone with the others.

Hesper trotted along behind her mother, filled with a sense of im-portance and drama. By Lovis Cove they met her father hurrying to-wards them, his thin face anxious, his vague eyes peering into their faces.

"What is it, Susan? Why didn't you tell me there was news?"

The child watched them, nervously expecting her mother's ready anger, because Pa had somehow failed again. But Susan was even quieter than she had been on the wharf. She laid her hand on her hus-band's arm. "Come back home, dear."

He gave her a startled, uncertain look, as surprised by this gentleness as Hesper was. They moved away from the child, and though Susan's hand still rested on her husband's arm, it was as though he leaned on her, his long body drooped over the broad figure beside him.

Hesper trailed after them. She paused at Fort Beach a moment to watch a sea-gull catch a fish, and felt a rough hand on her hair and a painful tug.

"Don't," she cried, whirling around, tears smarting her eyes. Two boys had crept up behind her—Johnnie Peach and Nathan Cubby. It was the latter who had pulled her hair, and he now began to caper around her jeering: "Gnaw your bacon, gnaw your bacon—little Fire-top's head is achin'."

Nat was a skinny boy of eleven, with watery yellow eyes and a sharp nose. Already Hesper was used to being teased about her flaming red hair, but she had not yet learned any defence. She shrank into herself, and tried to keep the tears from rolling out of her eyes.

"Oh, let her be," said Johnnie carelessly. "She's just a little kid."

He was a year younger than Nat, a handsome boy with curly dark hair. He shied a stone at the water and watched it skip.

"What for you're blubberin'—Fire-top?" taunted Nat, coming closer. "Blubberin' 'cause your head's on fire?" He made another grab at her hair.

Hesper ducked. "I'm crying 'cause Tom and Willy's gone down with the fleet," she wailed.

Johnnie turned. He raised his arm and struck down Nat's out-stretched hand. "That's so," he said. "They was on the *Liberty*. My uncle's lost, too, on the *Clinton*. Reason enough to cry without you roiling her."

"Oh, whip!" said Nat contemptuously, using an obscene Marble-head expletive. "I betcha my Pa's lost, too. Leastways, he hasn't come in from the spring fare yet. Ma, I think she's given him up."

Young as Hesper was, she was conscious of an obliquity in Nat, and that his speech about his father sprang from something stranger than bravado or the callousness of childhood. Though he was of normal height for his age, he had a hunched and wizened look and malicious, brooding eyes. He reminded her of a picture of an evil dwarf in the Grimms' *Fairy Tales* her father had given her.

"You shouldn't talk like that," said Johnnie severely, "and you shouldn't say 'whip' in front of a little lass. Run along home, Fire-top."

Hesper caught her under-lip with her teeth, though she didn't much mind the hated nickname from Johnnie. She looked at him adoringly, but the two boys had lost interest in her. They had sighted Peter Union's dory pulling around the rocks to his landing, and they clam-bered down to the beach to see what luck the fisherman had had.

Hesper wiped her face on a corner of her white muslin pinafore, threw the trailing ends of her shawl over her shoulders in a gesture duplicating her mother's, and continued homeward. The old house awaited her, and she thought, as she often had when approaching it from the water-side, that it looked like a great friendly mama cat. Its unpainted clapboards had weathered through two centuries to a tawny silver, and the huge brick chimneys, one on the old wing, one on the new, stuck up like ears. And the sign above the taproom door swung back and forth like a cat's tongue. There had once been painted em-blems on the sign, a pair of andirons and a flying bird above the letters "The Hearth and Eagle"; but they had all faded into a rusty red blur.

Hesper, moved by a feeling of special solemnity, went through the east door under the sign instead of around to the kitchen entrance as usual. The taproom door was closed, but she could hear her mother's voice, slow and thick with long pauses. So Ma and Pa were shut in there. Hesper wandered into the kitchen. It was still warm with the sunlight from the windows over the sink, but there were clouds building and the wind rising on the harbour.

Beside a fire in the great hearth, Gran sat huddled in her Boston rocking-chair. She was wrapped in fleecy grey shawls, and she looked like a tiny old sea-gull. Her black eyes were sea-gull eyes, too. "What's Roger doin' in the taproom with Susan?" she asked querulously when she saw Hesper. "And why'd he run out before?" Her voice was high and thin, but on a good day like this it had a snap to it.

"There's been a tor-rible thing happen to the fleet," said Hesper importantly, imitating Captain Chadwick. "Tom and Willy aren't never coming back. Ma's telling Pa."

The old woman's wrinkled eyelids hooded her eyes. She stopped rocking. "They ain't never coming back?" she repeated, seeming to consider. Her eyes opened and stared unseeing at the child. Her mouth drew itself into a pucker. "No more did Richard. He didn't come back." She shook her head. Her gaze slipped around the bright kitchen to rest on the hooked rug by the entry. "Right there I stood when I last saw Richard. I hooked that rug myself. Ship and sunset we called it."

Hesper obediently stared at the rug on which she had walked a thousand times. "It's real pretty," she said; then drew in her breath. There was a queer noise from the taproom. A broken cluttered sound like someone was crying, and mixed with it Ma's voice, firm and comforting. Pa was crying, thought the child in amazement, when he hadn't seemed worried at all about Tom and Willy before. The sounds frightened her, and she puzzled over them until she found the answer. It wasn't that Pa didn't feel, it was that he lived so far away he didn't believe in real things, and when they happened he didn't know what to do, except turn to Ma and let her comfort him.

Old Sarah Honeywood did not hear the sounds from the taproom. She kept on staring at the rug, and the misty present dissolved into the vivid emotion of seventy years ago, emotion she had thought long outrun, and yet it was still strong enough to rush forward again and overpower the changed body and the dim mind.

She saw Richard as he had stood that July day, boyish and handsome in his regimentals. The "handsomest man in Essex County," she had said to herself—that long-forgotten Sally Hathaway when Richard first came a-wooing to her father's house in Cunny Lane. She had said it again on the rug, her arms around his neck, the tears running down her face on to her red linsey-woolsey. With the memory of the red linsey-woolsey, the scene grew sharper and brighter. From outside she heard the shouts of the other men in Glover's regiment. Orders had just come from General Washington, saying the Marbleheaders must proceed to New York. Already half of them had sailed over to Beverley. Richard must hurry, yet she clung to him, begging and sobbing. He hadn't wanted to leave her, an eight-months' bride, and carrying his child. Yet he had been in high spirits.

14

"Us Marbleheaders'll show the stinking Red-coats how to fight, show the rest of them quiddling farmers too from back country. And so be it they've water down around New York we'll show 'em what a boat's for, too." He had said that even while he kissed her again, and pulled her clinging hands down from his neck.

"Fare ye well, Sally lass—I'll be back by snowfall."

But he hadn't come back. He had helped row the retreat from Brooklyn to New York after the dreadful battle of Long Island, and he had written her a letter, cocky as ever—"We saved the army, us Marbleheaders, we muffled the ors and rowed the poor lubbers acrost that little mill-pond they got down here-along. Don't fret, sweethart. It'll be over with soon."

How long had she kept that letter sewn into her bodice? Years it must have been, because she had nursed little Tom for two years, and long after that the letter was still in her bodice. It was the only letter she had ever got from Richard.

The Marbleheaders had rowed again on the night of December 25th. The old woman, caught by a single-minded urgency, got out of the rocker and walked gropingly towards her own room, the warm kitchen bedroom near the great chimney. In the bottom drawer of the pine dresser she unearthed, beneath piles of flannel nightcaps, an ancient tea-box, its purple roses and green daisies still glowing on the black lid after seventy years. Richard's letter was inside, tied up with black ribbon and rosemary; but it was not that she wanted. She shuffled through other keepsakes until she found a yellowed newspaper clipping. It was headed "Speech by General Knox," and she held it at arm's length, squinting her eyes.

"I wish the members of this body knew the people of Marblehead as well as I do. I could wish that they had stood on the banks of the Delaware River in 1776 in that bitter night when the Commander-in-Chief had drawn up his little army to cross it, and had seen the powerful current bearing onward the floating masses of ice which threatened destruction to whosoever should venture. . . ."

The remembered anguish of a few minutes ago gave place to the old thrill of pride. Sorrow was a solitary business, but pride must be shared. She put the clipping on her knee, and called the child.

"Hessie—I want you should come here."

Hesper obeyed slowly, a little rebellious. The strange noise in the taproom had stopped, and she had been amusing herself seeing pictures in the fire, the red leaping castles peopled by tiny golden fairies.

"I want you should listen to this. Set down, child."

The high quavering voice read the first paragraph out loud, and went on from Knox's speech. " 'I wish that when this occurrence threatened to defeat the enterprise, they could have heard that distinguished warrior demand, "Who will lead us on?" . . .' That was General Washington speakin', Hessie."

Hesper's attention came back with a jerk. She nodded politely. The clipping trembled in Gran's hand. "And you listen what Knox says next. 'It was the men of Marblehead, and Marblehead alone, who stood forward to lead the army along the perilous paths to unfading glories and honours in the achievements of Trenton. There went the fishermen of Marblehead, alike at home on land or water, alike ardent, patriotic and unflinching, whenever they unfurled the flag of the country.'"

The long words meant nothing to the child, but she was impressed by the way Gran looked, shining as if somebody'd lighted a candle behind her face.

"Richard was the first port oarsman right back of Washington, Bill Blackler commanded the boat. Josh Orne told me all about it months later. He said there was Richard, the sweat freezin' on his face, and cussin' something dreadful, but tryin' to swallow his oaths on account of General Washington there."

The old woman gave a sudden cackle of laughter. "Richard was a terrible one for bad language. Anything he didn't like, he'd yell, 'To hell I pitch it, and let the devil fry it on his rump!' I used to beg him to talk gentle, but pretty soon I give up." She sighed. "But he was a good boy."

Hesper frowned, struggling with a new impression. Gran often told stories, often changed like this, going from sad to glad so they didn't make much sense. Half the time she didn't listen. But something in the way Gran had said "He was a good boy" made it real.

The child put her hand on the bony grey knee. "Who was Richard, Gran?" The old woman twisted her head. An immense futility engulfed her. Explanations—why didn't people know without being told, why didn't anyone remember. . . .

"He was your—no, he was your *great* grand-sir, I guess," she said dully. "And he was killed at the Battle of Trenton."

Killed, thought Hesper. A queer word. A quick rippling word, it didn't sound very scary. Not like drowned—that was heavy and black.

Sarah had been wandering back again, not to clear-cut scenes, but to a long confusion of strivings. The striving to give birth here in this room—give birth to Tom. And forty years later his own hopeless striving for life, there on this very bed. Then the striving to make a living, running the tavern alone, until Tom grew up enough to help before he went off fishing with the bankers as a cut-tail. And another striving to give life, in this old Birth and Death room, the night Roger was born, and the niminy-piminy daughter-in-law, Mary Ellis, whimpering she couldn't get through it. Nor did she. Death again. Open and shutting, open and shutting the door of this room. I wish it'd open for me, she thought, I'm getting mighty weary. And she looked at the long cradle which stood in the corner of the room. Built two hundred years ago for Mark, the first Honeywood, who had something wrong with his spine. Rocking would soothe him, 'n it soothes me, too. In the cradle you could let go all this memory of striving, the beautiful grey peace folded over you, you floated back and forth, back and forth in the grey peace, and sometimes the rocking brought your mother's voice humming a soft little spinning song—and sometimes it brought Richard's voice singing above the lap of waves against a boat in the harbour.

"He sang real nice," she said out loud, and she began to quaver:

> "A pretty fair maid, all in a garden
> A sailor-boy came passing by
> He stepped aside and thus addressed her,
> Saying 'Pretty fair maid, won't you be my bride?'"

"Gran!" cried Hesper, tugging at the old woman's arm, for Gran had got up, still singing, and was going towards the long cradle. Her eyes had sunk back in her head and there was a silly little smile on her face. She was sliding into one of the bad times, when she wasn't Gran at all, just a helpless old baby wanting to be rocked.

"Gran," the child repeated urgently, "don't get in the cradle—Tom and Willy are drownded."

The old woman paused, the appeal in the child's voice reached her. Tom and Willy are drownded. Tom and Willy? She groped through the clinging grey peace, and shook her head, half in annoyance that the child's voice was detaining her, half in sympathy. "Well, don't take on, dearie. There's a many drownded here, and off the Banks too. Hark! I can hear the keel gratin' on the sand, that's what folks used to say, when death's comin' for them."

Death—the cool soft greyness floating down through peaceful waters that rocked you back and forth.

Hesper saw that the answering look had gone from Gran's face. Shaking off the child's hand, she climbed painfully into the long high cradle. She settled down with a sigh like a swish of wind through leaves.

"Rock Sally," she whispered plaintively. "Sally wants to be rocked."

Hesper looked down at the small face on the pillow beneath the sheltering oak hood. The wrinkles were smoothed away, the lips smiling in a secret and remote anticipation.

The child put her foot on the rocker and gave it one sharp push, but misery welled up from her tight chest. She jerked away from the cradle and stumbled into the kitchen.

Gran had gone back to her secret world. Ma and Pa were together behind a closed door. They were talking about Tom and Willy. It was an awful bad thing had happened. But I'm here, she thought, don't they care that I'm here?

She crept on to her special stool on the hearth inside the fireplace, and leaned her head against the bricks, sobbing quietly.

The small flames kept shimmering and dissolving between the huge andirons; the black balls that topped the andirons stood quiet above the noisy little fire like two proud, strong people. She watched the andirons, and her sobs lessened as she began to think about them. Pa and Gran used to talk of them sometimes, though Ma thought they were dreadful ugly and liked the brass ones in the parlour lots better. Pa called these tall black andirons Phebe's fire-dogs. Phebe'd brought them on a ship across the sea, so long ago that there wasn't any Marblehead here at all. Phebe was Mark Honeywood's wife. The first American Honeywood, Pa always said, though nobody ever would listen except Hesper. Most everyone in Marblehead had families that went way back, too.

But Pa thought there was something very special about Phebe, because of a letter. Pa said a great lady had written it, and it was something to be very proud of. He kept it wrapped in a yellow Chinese silk square in a carved wooden box in the secret drawer of his desk. He'd read it to Hesper on her last birthday; but she hadn't understood it very well, even though he made her repeat some of the phrases about being brave. "She hath a most sturdy courage" and "It is such as she who will endure in my stead."

Hesper had been much more interested in the embroidered yellow silk and the black box carved with the faces of slant-eyed men. These had belonged to Moses Honeywood, Pa's great-great-grandsir, who had owned three schooners in the China trade, and made a lot of money. The only Honeywood who had.

But Pa wouldn't let her play with the box, and he kept on talking about Phebe and Mark. He spoke of them as heroes and gods, comparing Mark to Odysseus and Phebe to a radiant all-conquering Hera. Sometimes he was bad as Gran, making her listen to old stories when she wanted to be playing hide-and-seek between the fish houses with Charry Trevercombe.

Hesper watched the andirons and the small leaping tongues of fire between them, when suddenly a thought struck her with the thrill of revelation. It was over two hundred years since Phebe brought those andirons here, but she must have sat just like this sometimes and watched them, too. Phebe was dead—all those others after her—Isaac and Moses and Zilpah and Richard, and now Tom and Willy, too. They were all dead. But the andirons were still just the same. They're letting *me* watch them now, she thought, with awe. Then there were some things like the fire-dogs—the letter, the house itself—that went on and on even if people did die. Things that didn't draw away from you and leave you alone the way people did. Things that didn't change from day to day. Miss Ellison, at Sabbath school, said God didn't either. But you couldn't touch and see God.

She frowned, struggling with a further concept. For had not Phebe and Mark, being dead, become as enduring as the andirons? Neither could they change now, and yet it was because of what they had been that Hesper, sitting by the hearth in the old house, was as she was.

Pa had said something like this when he read her the letter; but she had not understood. Now a great yearning came to her.

What were they like, Phebe and Mark? Why did they come here? What made the great lady write the letter?

She rested her head against the brick facing, and her eyelids drooped. But it seemed to her that on the flagstone hearth she saw the image of a ship, the size of the schooners in the harbour but of a strange and quaint rig. And it seemed to the child that on the deck of this ship she saw the figure of a girl in blue. She could not really see the girl's face, and yet Hesper knew that there were tears on it. Frightened, anguished tears, and this seemed strange to her, for she knew the girl was Phebe, and did such brave people cry or shrink like that?

Hesper sighed, and the image on the hearthstone blurred and faded. Her head fell forward on her chest, and she slept. Outside, the nor'easter ripped up the harbour, piling the leaden waves against the wharves and causeway. The rising storm brought restlessness and danger in its whistling blasts, but the house gathered around to protect the yearning dreams of still another Honeywood.

CHAPTER TWO

(The Beginning—1630)

THE rising wind brought restlessness and a sense of danger. Already Phebe Honeywood had learned that. It brought the crudest physical misery as well. Phebe raised her swimming head above the wooden rim of their bunk and groped again for the tin basin.

The *Jewell* rolled and lurched and rolled once more, and Phebe, still retching, fell back on the straw pallet. Mark had risen long ago and gone off to the fo'c'sle with the crew. These shipboard days he was always eager and interested as she had never yet seen him in their six months of marriage, nor was he seasick.

From the bunk above Phebe, Mistress Brent gave a long groan, followed by a grunt from her husband and little Rob's wail. There were three of them up there, wedged into a bunk like their own, which, as Mark said cheerfully, was "sized exactly to a coffin." But they had been fortunate to get space in the only small cabin. The other fifty passengers slept as best they could on layers of rickety shelves in the great cabin, or in hammocks between decks.

This was Friday, April 9th; they had been twelve days at sea and not yet quitted England, still near the Isle of Wight. Dead calms and adverse winds had prevented. Twelve days of cold and bad food and seasickness, and the journey not begun. It seemed to Phebe that already twelve weeks had passed since she kissed her father farewell and boarded the *Jewell* at Southampton, where she lay in the Channel with the other three ships in this vanguard of Governor Winthrop's fleet—the *Talbot*, the *Ambrose* and their beautiful flagship, the *Arbella*.

Phebe raised her head again, then inched gingerly to a crouching position. The dark cabin swirled around her, and she leaned her head against the rough planking. She heard Mark's laugh from the deck outside and he burst into the cabin.

"What, Phebe," he cried between laughter and reproach, peering into their dark bunk, "not puking again?"

Over feeble protests from the sufferers in the top berth he flung open the wooden shutter of the deck window, to let wind and grey light rush through the noisome cabin.

"Aye, you do look green, poor lass," he said, examining his wife.

"But you should cheer now. We've a fair wind at last. Come, dress yourself—we'll soon be passing Portland Bill."

She tried to smile up at him, this great, swaggering, handsome youth in his red leather doublet, so tall that he must keep his dark curly head bent low to stand in the cabin. She loved him dearly, but his words brought her lacerating pain which he would never understand. Portland Bill was but a few miles from Dorchester—from home.

If they must leave England, she thought, turning her face from him, why could it not be clean and sharp as they had thought in Southampton—instead of this long-drawn, ever-renewed parting?

Mark, seeing her hesitant and thinking it the seasickness, scooped her from the bunk, stood her on the planks in her nightshift, and held up his scarlet cloak to screen her from the inert Brents above.

Phebe clenched her teeth and hurried through her dressing. Mark teased her for her modesty, but she suffered deeply at the public nature of all private acts on board the ship. She put on her everyday gown of French serge, blue as the cornflowers in the meadow at home, and her white lawn falling collar, whose points were embellished with rows of tucks, in elaboration exactly suitable to a prosperous yeoman's daughter. The collar was limp from the sea air and hung badly. Phebe sighed, thinking of the care her mother had lavished on fine linen for the journey.

Mark impatiently wrapped her in her blue, hooded cloak and hurried her out on deck.

The easterly wind had not brought rain, nor was it cold this April day, as the little *Jewell* bounded across the waves, seeming as eager as Mark was to hurtle herself towards the western sea and be quit of old England for ever.

There was scarce room to move on deck, since all the passengers who were well enough had come out to wedge themselves amongst the water barrels, the chicken coops and the long-boat, and they were heartily cursed by the harassed sailors. But there was no other place to take the air. Only Mark, by dint of his exuberant interest and treats of strong water to the crew, was allowed on the fore-deck, and Captain Hurlston permitted no one but his officers on the poop.

Phebe leaned against the starboard rail, her eyes on the shadowy coastline. She was always quiet, even in their moments of passionate love, but Mark's jubilance was checked by the expression of her face as they neared the headlands of Dorsetshire.

He put his arm around her. "Take heart," he whispered, bending down; for she was small and her smooth brown head barely reached to his shoulder. "It's a great venture, Phebe."

Her indrawn breath dilated her nostrils. Her fingers twisted in the folds of her cloak. "I know," she said.

How well she knew for him the restlessness, the discontent at home and the zest for the untried which had all compelled him to this venture. His nature was made for struggle. It had been so with their marriage. She had not loved as soon as he did, and her indifference had excited him as much as her father's opposition had angered him.

Mark's father was but a small Dorchester clothier, never prosperous, and of late oppressed by the new taxes, harried by imposts and restrictions to the verge of bankruptcy, while Phebe Edmunds was the child of a wealthy yeoman farmer, who was distantly connected with gentry, and freeholder of the same Dorsetshire acres which had been granted to his ancestor after the Conquest.

But when Phebe's love had at last grown strong as Mark's, her indulgent father's opposition wore itself out. Six months ago, on her eighteenth birthday, they had married and found great joy in each other. Yet she had known Mark still unsatisfied.

He detested Dorchester and the clothiers' trade to which he had never given but grudging attention anyway, preferring always the wharves and sea eight miles away at Weymouth. That she understood, but she long fought against another realization. Her own beloved home, the great sprawling half-timbered house set in gentle meadows and warm with the affection of a close-knit family—this he detested even more.

"Yet what is it you want so much?" she had cried, as she began to see the extent of his unrest. "What can New England give us better than we have here? It's not as though we were Separatists."

Mark's under-lip had jutted out in the stubborn way she had come to dread. "No need to be Puritan to build new and free in a new land." He had thrown a resentful glance around the Edmunds's great hall where they were sitting, at the sparkling casement windows newly curtained in a delicate rose sarsenet, at the carved oaken chairs, the gilded court cupboard, the polished floor-cloth painted like a chequer board and warmed by a Turkey rug.

"Soon, perhaps," she suggested timidly, "we can build for ourselves."

His face had blackened, and he flung his head up like a spurred stallion. "Aye, on your father's land! Where he'll o'ersee all I do." He jumped to his feet and began to pace the Turkey rug. "Look, Phebe. I mean to be my own master. Nor account for what I do to king or bishop or commissioner or father—yours or mine. I'll never make a clothier nor"—he glanced contemptuously towards the window—"nor sheep farmer."

Phebe's family after the first dismay had accepted Mark's plan. For was there not fear and insecurity everywhere, now that the King had rid himself of Parliament and gave ear to his Papist Queen who might yet force back the terrible days of Bloody Mary?

"Aye, times are mortal bad," Phebe's father agreed, wagging his grizzled head. "Were I younger, Phebe sweeting, I mought come with 'ee." Yet even as he spoke he cast a complacent look about his comfortable house and through the window to the rolling downs, dotted with his sheep. And she knew that come what might, her parents would never leave home. They would bend a little here and there under necessity, and conform to any order, secure in the hundreds of years which had rooted them to these acres and this life.

And I, too, she thought, as she had thought many times during the weeks of preparation; though once the decision had been taken she had never troubled Mark with her doubts. Her love for him deepened as they became isolated together by their shared enterprise. She listened anxiously while he spelled out the planter's list of requisites suggested by the Massachusetts Bay Company—bellows, scoop, pail, shovels, spades, axes, nails, fish-hooks and lines. All these were Mark's concern; for their purchase, and the passage money of six pounds each, and the freightage costs, he used most of the hundred pounds left him by his mother. To buy the remaining requisites, warm clothes, household gear and provisions, Phebe used her dowry, since Mark stubbornly refused any help proffered by his father-in-law.

In only one thing had she combated her husband's will. She had insisted upon bringing her wedding andirons. They had been made for her by a master blacksmith of more than local fame. They were tall and sturdy, fit to hold the greatest logs, yet graceful, too, in the deceptively slender shafts and the crowning black balls.

Fire-dogs were not on the planter's list.

"But I want them, Mark," she insisted, near tears. "I want them in our first hearth wherever it may be."

He had given in at last, though he had not understood. Only her mother had understood, that the andirons ordered in love for her by her parents to grace a new hearth would always be a link with home, the twin guardians of the precious flame; like man and wife. English-born, transplanted and yet enduring with steady purpose. But indeed those were womanish thoughts, unfitting to a man, and standing now on the *Jewell* deck beside him, she shifted her weight and pressed against him, glorying in his strength and bigness, waiting for the quick response of his arm to the pressure of her body.

But Mark was not thinking of love. He made a sharp movement, swinging on his heel, and stretching his hand above his head. "God blast, the bloody wind is slacking off again!"

She followed his scowling gaze up to the sails that now were flapping fitfully, where they had been taut-bellied before. She turned and looked again towards the land, and saw, jagged and sharp against the sky, the crenellations of Portland Castle where she and her sisters had played a hundred times, gathering moss-roses around the ruined walls, then galloping over the strip of shingle on their little moor ponies. Behind the castle and over that rounded ridge of hills—lay home. Mother would be in the still-room at this hour, sugaring the new cowslips for her famous wine, or maybe helping the dairymaids skim the cream. And painted clear against the sky Phebe saw the sweet comely face, rosy as an apple beneath the greying hair, heard the loving admonishments and the ready laughter. She'd had a bad cough when they left home a fortnight back, what if it had worsened and gone down into the lungs, what . . .

Phebe clutched at the wooden rail and shut her eyes.

"Satan himself must be in it," said Mark morosely, staring across the league of water to the north. "Back where we started. One might lower the long-boat, row ashore and be at your father's in a couple of hours."

"Oh, don't!" cried Phebe so loud and sharp that Mark started and gaped at her. She held her head rigidly turned from him, her small brown hands clenched on the rail, but beneath her cloak he saw her shoulders shaking.

He leaned over her with clumsy and puzzled tenderness. "Phebe—what ails you, sweetheart?"

She gathered herself tighter and whispered through her teeth, "Let me be. Let me be a while."

He patted her shoulder and left her, heading forward to the fo'c'sle.

After a few minutes the capricious wind returned, the sails filled and the *Jewell* gained headway. Phebe moved her body so that she might no longer see the diminishing shore, and stared ahead doggedly towards the other three ships of their company, all drifting still becalmed almost within hailing distance. She had no interest in the *Ambrose* and the *Talbot*; her brooding gaze rested on their flagship the *Arbella*, and gradually, as she fixed her thoughts on it, she felt a dawning solace.

The *Arbella* was by far the largest ship of them all, near 400 tons burden; she had been newly painted for the voyage in gay reds and whites and shining black, and her figurehead, the flying gilded eagle on her prow, glinted proudly in the uncertain sunlight. There were great folk aboard—Governor John Winthrop, who was to head their colony; Sir Richard Saltonstall and his children. These were gentry indeed, but she knew little of them except a glimpse in the distance when they embarked at Southampton. In the most noble passenger of all, however, Phebe felt vivid interest, because she had talked with her.

Three days ago whilst they still awaited favourable winds off the Isle of Wight, many from all four ships had put ashore at Yarmouth, that they might walk about and refresh themselves. Mark had been away at once, eager to explore the little town, but Phebe found no such energy. She was content to walk along the beach, relieved by the feeling of earth beneath her feet. She had wandered a short distance around the bend and up the mouth of the Yar when she came upon a low bank covered with beach grass and shaded by the ruin of an ancient look-out. She prepared to sit down on a block of fallen masonry, when she saw a young woman standing nearby. The woman was richly dressed in garnet-coloured paragon, somewhat stained with sea water, and beneath the fur-lined walking hood her shadowed blue eyes gazed out to sea with an expression of both yearning and resolution which touched immediate understanding in Phebe. She was too shy to accost a lady, obviously high-born and still further protected by intense preoccupation with her own thoughts. But the lady heard and, giving a slight start, turned. Seeing a girl some years younger than herself, staring with admiration, she smiled and made a gentle gesture of welcome. "You are on one of the ships, mistress?"

Phebe smiled too and curtsied. "Yes, your ladyship. From the *Jewell*."

"You know who I am?" asked the lady in some surprise.

"I guessed," said Phebe gently. "For I've heard that the Lady Arbella is tall, has golden hair and is fair as the mayflower."

Arbella withdrew a little. The words touched memory of many venal flatteries. But she examined the quiet young face upturned to hers, saw that the brown eyes were honest and clear as brook water, and she smiled again.

"Sit down, mistress, and tell me of yourself, since we are fellow-travellers."

Phebe hesitated. "I intrude, I fear. A moment alone is so precious now. Already I've learned that."

Arbella nodded and sighed, but checked herself. "Our gracious Lord has harder lessons than that in store for us, but with His Mercy we'll conquer."

Why, she is homesick as I am, thought Phebe with sharp sympathy. "It means much to us all to have you venture with us, your ladyship," said Phebe earnestly. "It gives us courage."

"Ah, child—only God can give you that." But Phebe saw that her words had pleased. Arbella took the girl's hand and drew her down on the stone beside her. "Are you with your husband, mistress? You're not truly of our Puritan congregation, since you wear a wedding-ring."

"No," said Phebe, glancing at the gold band on her finger, then at the lady's ringless hands. "Forgive me, but I can't think it wrong."

"Nor I," said Arbella faintly. "But it's a Papist symbol for all that, and we must purify our Church. My beloved husband thinks it very wrong," she added half to herself, thinking of Isaac and his burning zeal to cleanse their form of worship from corruption. He had denied himself even his hour's respite from the ship, and was now, as usual, closeted with Governor Winthrop, planning and praying for the success of their colony in the New World.

She turned to Phebe. "But tell me of yourself, mistress." She was much interested in this girl, who obviously came from a class she hardly knew. Neither gentry nor of the lower orders.

Phebe, always self-possessed, willingly answered Arbella's questions, and when she spoke of Mark, Arbella smiled, accurately building an image of a handsome, impetuous youth, eager for adventure, but well knowing how to hold a woman's love.

"But if it's not for conscience' sake he emigrates, what is it he hopes to find in the New England?" she asked at last, and Phebe, who had herself often been troubled by this question, found the answer promptly.

"Freedom, milady—and"—her lips parted in her rare smile—"and—I believe—fish."

"Fish! Is he then a fisherman by trade?"

"No, milady—a clothier, but he hates it. He has been much influenced by the clergyman, Master White at Dorchester, who believes that in fishing New England will find great fortune. Mark is drawn to the sea, he ever loved the docks and boats at Weymouth."

"But you—mistress," said Arbella, frowning. "You're bred to gentler ways. I cannot see you as a fishwife."

Phebe hesitated, fearing to seem forward. "I think, milady, there will be no gentle ways for anyone out there in the wilderness, no matter what we be."

A darkness deepened the lady's blue eyes. She rose from the stone. Phebe saw that the long pale hand which drew together her fur cloak wavered; but her answer was firm. "You're right. I pray that I may have the strength."

As they stood there, they heard the far-off boom of a cannon.

"The signal," said Arbella, turning slowly towards the water. "We must get back to the ships. With God's mercy, we shall meet again at Naumkeag. God keep you, mistress."

"And you, milady," said Phebe softly. She watched the tall, swaying figure walk down the beach, and she felt again the glow of pride she had tried to voice earlier. The Lady Arbella Johnson was the daughter and sister of an earl, the most noble Earl of Lincoln. What if many of the malcontents did now sneer at a title, what if the new dissenting creeds averred that all are equal in the sight of God, was there not special courage required of such a one as the Lady Arbella, sheltered, delicate and accustomed to delicacy? The first noblewoman to venture towards the New England. For conscience' sake, thought Phebe, docilely echoing the Puritan lady's own words. But from deep within her a surer voice spoke. Not only for conscience' sake, she goes for love of her husband—even as I.

As if in answer, she saw Mark racing down the beach towards her, waving his Monmouth cap, his curly dark hair disordered, his eyes alight. "Phebe—Phebe—hurry; the shallop's leaving. I couldn't find you."

Warmth and gladness at the sight of him rushed through her body; she held out her arms and he caught her hard against him, kissing her on the mouth. "A fair welcome, sweetheart. But hurry." She obediently ran with him down the beach, his arm around her waist. Those already waiting in the shallop eyed them sourly as they arrived, laughing, their cheeks flushed, and about them the glow of hot love.

Mistress Bagby, the midwife from London, made grudging room for Phebe on the afterthwart. "You pleasured yourself in Yarmouth?" she sniffed. "At a pothouse, maybe?"

Phebe shrugged, indifferent in this moment of new courage to the spiteful fat face beside her. "Nay, mistress. I only walked up the Yar a way, and there I met the Lady Arbella."

Mrs. Bagby stared, then masked her envy with another sniff. "And being noticed by quality has gone to your head, I see. I've heard, she's but a meaching, mincing thing."

"She is very fair and winsome and brave," said Phebe and, turning her back, looked over the other heads to the bow where Mark pulled on a larboard oar. He caught her eye and they smiled at each other.

This sureness and warmth between them sustained her that night through their first quarrel. As they lay cramped together in their bunk, she tried to tell of her meeting with the Lady Arbella, and he would not listen, speaking to her roughly and telling her that she was fool indeed to think that the daughter of an earl had shown true good-will. It was then that she remembered that he had cause to hate the lady's class. Once as a boy of eight he had snared a rabbit on lands belonging to the Earl of Dorset. He had been caught and punished by the earl's order, cruelly beaten and his left ear cropped. Of this he had never spoken but once. His abundant hair hid the jagged wedge-space cut from his ear, and she had forgotten.

She soothed him with soft murmurs and the tenderness of her body, but their disagreement was not yet ended. Mark, too, had something to tell of their stay in Yarmouth, and she felt sharp dismay when she found that he had spent some of their small horde of silver for a strange purchase.

He pulled his prize from under the straw at their feet, and made her feel sundry bumpy objects in the darkness.

"What are they?" she whispered, though the snoring of their cabin-mates, the creaking of the ship and the rush of water made secrecy needless.

"Lemons," he answered triumphantly, stuffing them back beneath the straw.

"Whatever for?" she cried. She had hoped at least for sugar-plums to vary the dreadful sameness of their food.

"I met an old sailor in Yarmouth; he's been fifty years at sea, to Cathay and back. He says if we suck one every day we'll not get ship fever. He sold them to me for eleven shillings."

"Oh, Mark—and you believed him! He was but diddling you to get the profit."

He drew his arm from under her. "They've come from Spain," he said with anger. "Lemons are always dear. You must not question my judgment, Phebe."

"No, Mark, I won't," she said after a minute, hurt that he had turned from her again. "Forgive me."

And she hid her worry. For it seemed to her ordered mind that his buying of the lemons touched things in him that her love would rather forget, a recklessness and improvidence.

But after they had at last bade final farewell to England, and the journey became a plodding, ever-recurrent nightmare of storm and sickness, it did seem that she and Mark were stronger than many of the others.

All over the ship the passengers complained of sharp pains in their bones, of swollen mouths and tongues, and teeth so weak they could not chew upon the hard salt meat the cabin-boy flung into the wooden trenchers. She and Mark had none of this, and now that her young body had become accustomed to the pitching and tossing of the ship, even seasickness no longer bothered her.

On May Day during a great storm and cold, Phebe helped a frantic mother tend her sick child in the great cabin, and while she wiped the little girl's swollen blue lips, she mentioned hesitantly the lemons. "I don't know if they do good, but Mark thinks so and we *have* kept well."

Mrs. Bagby had also been tending the child, and now she hooked her fat arm around the upright of a bunk to keep her feet on the lurching floor, and said scornfully, "Lemons forsooth! You think the child doesn't suffer enough already, Mistress Honeywood, that you must parch her poor mouth. Give her beer, Goody Carson, beer and wormwood. That'll help her."

And Goody Carson listened to the midwife, who was a determined woman of reputed skill; for Goody Carson was big with child and near to term, and she feared that she would need Mrs. Bagby's good-will before the journey was over.

Phebe said nothing more. She was unsure herself if those shrivelling acid little fruits were contributing to their health, but each morning before they pulled themselves out of the damp, mouldering bunk straw, Mark split two lemons with his hunting-knife, and they sucked and swallowed the bitter pulp.

The journey went on and the weeks went by. Long since the memory of home had faded to a haze as unreal as the impossible visioning of the future scene. Nobody thought of either. The ship life alone was true and its incidents the only interest. Bad food, increasingly scanty, bad weather, bad smells, bad air and bitter cold. These made the dun thread on which the days slid by; but now and then it seemed to knot itself and pause for a more vivid pattern. There was the Sabbath service, held on deck if the weather permitted, or, as it usually did not, in the great cabin, smoky from the cook-fire and stinking from some fifty unwashed bodies. On the *Jewell* there was no ordained minister, but a godly little clerk, Master Wenn, from Norwich, made shift to read the Bible, lead the prayers and even preach. Mark always escaped the services; being welcomed by the sailors, where he listened to sea-lore instead. But Phebe perforce listened with the other passengers, and was much irritated by the canting nasal voice. She missed the candles and the rituals and prayers to which she was accustomed, and found Master Wenn's bald manner of exhorting God shocking in its crudeness. But this and many other matters she kept to herself.

In mid-Atlantic a sailor died, one who had been increasingly drunk and blasphemous, and many thought it a judgment on him and were pleased.

It was a matter of comfort, too, that usually they were in sight of the other ships—the *Arbella* and the *Ambrose*, though the *Talbot* had disappeared after they left the Scillies. Phebe would sometimes push her way to one of the square portholes in the great cabin, and gaze across the heaving grey waters to the *Arbella*, thinking of the beautiful lady who was the ship's namesake, and wondering how she endured the hardships. It seemed that the ships made no progress, gales and storms followed one another; the passengers, forbidden the deck for fear of pounding waves, became some quarrelsome, some apathetic.

On Thursday, May 27th, came a day of special trial. They had been seven weeks on the open sea, all night a stiff gale had harried them. The little *Jewell* climbed the mountainous waves, shivering as if in fear at the summit, then pitching down to drive her prow a fathom through green water. All night Phebe had clung to Mark, while his long legs braced against the sides of their bunk, and at dawn they dragged themselves to the great cabin for food, both bruised and dizzy. The glum faces of the few passengers who were on their feet announced a new disaster. The beer had given out. Nothing to drink but the slimy, fetid water which all knew was unwholesome. "We must ask Captain Hurlston to broach us a cask of spirits," said Mark; "that alone can make the water safe."

The others nodded and murmured. The sailors had beer, but their supplies, too, were running low, and to deprive them had caused mutiny at sea before this.

The gale had continued, and now the rain sliced like silver knives at the rigging. By noon the cold in the cabin was bitter as winter. Teeth chattered and faces turned blue and pinched. Many coughed from the smoke of the cook-fire, which could not escape through the closed portholes.

For dinner there was the watery pease porridge in which floated chunks of salt beef. Most had no appetite, and Phebe gave her portion to one of the young boys.

In mid-afternoon Mark came in with news. Since the sailor's death, he and another passenger had been pressed into filling some seaman duties. The *Arbella* had managed to send over a skiff to borrow a hogshead of meal, and in return had sent back brandy. There was a feeble cheer, and anxious faces lightened a little.

By dusk all had forgotten themselves in pity and a new fear. Goodwife Carson suddenly started into active labour. Mrs. Bagby kept her head and habit of firm command, but matters were not going right. The labouring woman's shrieks tore through the main cabin, even after Phebe, horrified by the public exposure of the poor woman's ordeal, had helped to carry her to her own bunk in the small cabin. Two of the older women followed, crowding close in the cold, airless space, trying to help the midwife. Anguish and death crowded with them. Helpless, they watched the agonized body wracked not only by labour pains but by the violent tossing of the ship, too. In an instant between pains the woman lifted her head, the hair matted and wet, the eyes like an animal's. "Can ye not make it still an instant?" she wailed. "An it were quiet an instant, I might . . ." But a wave so big hit the ship that her body was flung against the bulkhead, and again that thin animal scream splintered the air.

Phebe, repulsed by the midwife, stumbled into the great cabin and, going to the latrine bucket, vomited a little. I must get out, she thought. I must. And running to the ladder, she climbed it and pushed with all her strength against the hatch above. She pounded on it frantically. It would not move. She crouched on the upper step, clinging to the rail. The dreadful screams were growing weaker.

"She can't endure," thought Phebe. In the great cabin a steady murmuring had begun. She lifted her head and listened. Master Wenn was reading from the Bible.

Above the hissing of the waves, the creaking of the joists and the groans from the cabin, she heard the nasal voice intoning:

"Unto the woman he said, I will greatly multiply thy sorrow and thy conception; in sorrow thou shalt bring forth children; and thy desire shall be to thy husband. . . ."

THAT will not help her, thought Phebe, with sudden hot anger. She ran down the ladder and burst in on them, the little group of women and children and a few shamefaced men who listened.

"Can you do nothing for her besides *pray*!" she cried.

They stared at her; Mistress Honeywood had seemed always so composed and aloof.

Mr. Wenn rested the ponderous Bible on his lap, his tight little face with its peaked grey beard seemed to consider her. His eyes were unexpectedly kindly. He did not rebuke her for interrupting the word of God, even though he disapproved of the Honeywoods as irreligious, careless conformists.

"And what can we do for her but pray, mistress?" he asked quietly.

The anger left Phebe and she bowed her head.

"I don't know," she whispered. "Forgive me." She shivered and, drawing her cloak tight around her, sank on the edge of a bench.

Master Wenn bent his head again to the Bible, screwing up his eyes to see the text by the flickering light of the iron lanthorn. Phebe tried to fix her mind on the droning voice, but she could not. From the small cabin now there came at times a long choking moan. Phebe's hands gripped each other and she floundered through the black wash of fear. Fear for Goody Carson, that stupid but well-tempered woman reduced now to a thing less than human—and that other fear which she had not dared face. I, too, next February maybe—like that creature in there. No—it is but the hardships have delayed me. I cannot have conceived in that bunk where she lies now, conceived in the mouldy straw—the lice—the ignoble stealthiness, watchful even in the unguarded ecstasy because the Brents might hear.

The ships lurched onward through the falling night, though the howling of the wind had abated, and the motion. On the deck above her head heavy footsteps passed. She heard the muffled shout of orders.

Around Master Wenn a group still listened, their heads bowed. Phebe looked down at her wedding-ring, and into the confusion of fear there came the thought of the Lady Arbella. *She* would not give way like this, possessed of inner panic, resentful that her husband did not somehow divine a need and fly from man's work to comfort her. The Lady Arbella was strong and invincible.

Phebe moistened her dry lips, got off the bench and went to the fire. No one had thought to replenish it, and the logs had fallen apart to smouldering ash. Yet food must be cooked for the children.

Her head throbbed as she bent over, but she shovelled the ashes into a heap, careful not to disturb the thick coating of dirt and brick dust which protected the wooden planking under the fire. She studied to lay each stick of pitchy kindling fair and square. As she finished and the flames, aided by wind from the bellows, crackled upward to the oak logs, a new sound came from the small cabin which had long been quiet. The acrid cry of the new-born.

Master Wenn closed his Bible. They all pressed through the door. Mrs. Bagby met them triumphantly. Her falling band was stained with blood, her fat face haggard, her hair in wisps. She held a swaddled bundle. "A girl. Never have I so needed my skill."

"But the mother," cried Phebe, staring at the still mound.

"She'll do," Mrs. Bagby shrugged, put the baby at the foot of the bunk. "Fair lot o' trouble she gave me. Has the strong-water been broached?"

A sigh ran over them all. The moment of unity passed, they fell apart into their separate groups. Master Wenn and the two old men went to find the brandy. The children fell to quarrelling beneath the ladder.

Most of the women gathered around, asking the midwife eager questions, while she cleansed herself a little in a cask of sea water.

Phebe had no taste for spirits, but when the brandy came she helped the others to mix it with the river water they had taken at Yarmouth, and like them drank thirstily from the dipper.

Later, when Mark appeared at last, bringing with him the freshness of damp sea air, she had hidden all trace of her fears.

Mark was in high spirits and full of the day's happenings on deck. The skiff from the *Arbella* had nearly foundered on her perilous trips between the two ships, but the wind had turned in the nick of time. They kept fairly well on board there, though many were dying on the *Ambrose*.

"And the Lady Arbella herself?" asked Phebe, braving Mark's displeasure. But he was in an indulgent mood. "I dare say she bears up like the rest," he said carelessly. "I heard nothing contrary. Is that woman and her brat to have our bunk?" He looked towards their cabin.

Phebe nodded. "We can't turn them out tonight."

"Well. Then I must have me another noggin, and you too, 'twill soften our couch."

Phebe was grateful for the brandy haze as they lay down on the planking wedged into a space between a hogshead of dried pease and the forward bulkhead. The stink of the bilges was stronger here, and a rat scuttled about their feet. Mark put his arm close around her, and she lay with her head on his shoulder, trying to doze. But she could not.

The brandy and the stench brought back the seasickness she had thought conquered.

"Why must the ship for ever roll so?" she whispered plaintively, trying to control her twitching stomach and thinking Mark asleep.

"Why, it's your thrice-damned fire-dogs, poppet," he answered, chuckling. "No doubt they overbalance the ship, didn't you know that?"

She forgot her stomach, happy that he should tease her, glad that she had forborne to trouble him with the panic and forebodings she had suffered.

Ah, we will endure, she thought, and all be well. It can't be for much longer. And she closed her eyes.

30

But the journey went on. Another week of cold and sudden gales and calms passed by. There was more sickness, not only the frequent purging and gripes in the belly from which all suffered at times, but an epidemic of feverish colds that left its victims with a strangling cough and a purulent discharge from the nose. The daily food rations shrank; but few cared, for the pork had spoiled, the stringy hunks of beef induced a thirst which there was no beer to quench, and the hard biscuits were coated with blue mould. They lived on pease-porridge and water-gruel.

Goody Carson, the new mother, was up from child-bed, but her wits seemed befuddled; she neither spoke nor smiled, and she had scanty milk for her nursling, whose wails were incessant. The baby had been named Travail, and as the passengers' tempers grew ever shorter, there was many an acid jest as to the appropriateness of its naming.

Everywhere on the ship small feuds had risen. Master Wenn led a clique of Separatists who joined in disapproval of those whose reasons for emigrating were not primarily religious.

Mrs. Bagby, from malice and boredom, headed another faction held together by resentment towards Phebe, because she kept herself apart, because she was young and more gently bred than they, because she wore a small lace ruff around her neck on Sundays, because she and her wild young gawk of a husband—naught but a tradesman either—seemed set far from the rest by a wanton show of passion for each other.

Phebe heard the whispers and knew herself shunned, but she was too weary and indifferent to care. She silently took her turn at the communal duties, the cooking of whatever food the cabin-boy flung in the trenchers, the emptying of chamber-pots and slop-pails, the care of the sick, and otherwise lived for the moments of dubious privacy in the bunk with Mark. She had not told him of her private fear, shamed that she should think it a fear. Besides, as long as it remained unvoiced, it remained unreal. And there might yet be a mistake. Time enough to face it when they reached land. *If* they reached land. That was the thought in all their hearts. Day after day the soundings touched no bottom. Day after day the endless ocean stretched on ahead. And then one day they could no longer see the water, for an icy grey fog, colder and thicker than any they had met before, swathed the *Jewell* in a sinister quiet. The incessant blare of the horn sounded muffled and impotent and no sound came back except the purling of the sea at the barely moving bow.

The passengers, at first relieved to find steady decks beneath their feet, soon caught the contagion of renewed and sharper anxiety. The sailors had turned surly and would not speak. Captain Hurlston, briefly glimpsed on the poop-deck, kept thereafter to his quarters in the round house, and returned no answers to anxious messages.

Even Mark lost his optimism, and from his few glum words Phebe learned their peril. They must be near the Grand Banks, there were dangerous shoals to the south. They had lost the other ships four days ago, and in the fog the captain was unsure of his bearings.

No, Mark answered impatiently to her frightened question, of course there was nothing further to be done, except wait. "And I dare say you women and Master Wenn might pray on't." He escaped soon to the fo'c'sle, where at least there were no foolish questions, and where he had become proficient at knots and splices and learned the knack of the marlin-spike.

The fog continued that night and on into the next day, which was June 6th and colder than any January day in Dorset. After a basin of porridge, Phebe lay down in her bunk, shivering. The matted straw pallet beneath her was damp as a dish-cloth, and seemed to have vanquished even the lice, which were less troublesome. She lay wrapped in her cloak and with their two bed-rugs piled on top. She shut her eyes tight, trying to escape for a while into sleep, when she heard the thumps of running feet on the deck and men's voices raised in a resounding cheer. "Land ho! Huzzah! Huzzah!"

She jumped from the berth and went out on deck.

The fog had suddenly lifted beneath a pale watery sun, and far off to the north rose a black line of cliff. Her heart swelled with wild relief. "Oh, thank God it's Naumkeag!" she cried, crowding with the other excited passengers to the starboard rail.

"No, sweetheart." She turned to see Mark laughing at her. "You push us too fast. It's Cape Sable, and many days yet ahead of us. But it is the New World at last!" He bent down and kissed her exuberantly, unnoticed for once by Mrs. Bagby and Master Wenn, who were united in the general elation.

They were indeed off the Grand Banks, the famous fishing banks to which European boats had been sailing for centuries. And the sea being most providently quiet, they lay to while the sailors and most of the male passengers commenced to fish. They were abundantly rewarded: in less than two hours they had taken near fifty giant codfish. The women retreated to the poop-deck, as the main deck became a mass of silvery flopping bodies. Phebe watched Mark, and ignorant as she was of the art, saw that he seemed more apt than the other landsmen. His movements in casting out the hand-line were quicker, he seemed to know by instinct the moment for the sharp jerk, he caught more fish than they did, and he caught the biggest of all—a yard long and near to that around the middle.

She thought of the Lady Arbella's remark, "I cannot see you as a fishwife," and smiled inwardly. And far across the water to the south-west the *Arbella* lay ahead of them, also hove-to, and doubtless also fishing. Later, when they had glutted themselves with the sweet fresh fish, so delicious a change in their fare, she thought of Arbella again, and said to her mentally, "You do not despise the occupation so now, do you, milady?"

The fish were good omen, not only for the bodies which they strengthened, but for the voyage. The winds at last grew fair and the weather warm. Off to starboard high land and mountains streamed by. All might spend the day on deck in the sunshine, and pleasant sweet air drifted to them from the land, like the smell of a garden.

The strain relaxed from Mr. Hurlston, the ship's master, and he who had been grimly aloof during those endless weeks at sea grew and gladly pointed out to them the landmarks they passed. Desert, Agamenticus, the Isle of Shoals. Off Cape Ann a stiff south-west gale delayed them, but now so near to land and having weathered so many worse gales, the passengers scarcely minded.

On June 13th, the Lord's Day, the *Jewell* slid gingerly through the passage between Baker's Isle and Little Isle, and at two o'clock the whole ship's company again let forth a mighty cheer, for there to the north of them, rocking at anchor, rested the *Arbella*, seeming as placid and at home as she had seemed so many weeks ago in Southampton harbour.

"And THAT is Naumkeag," cried Phebe, staring with all her eyes at the wooded shore behind the *Arbella*.

"Nay, Phebe," said Mark, laughing as he had laughed a week earlier when she miscalled Cape Sable. He took her by the shoulders and swung her around toward the south-east. "Down there is Naumkeag. Here is Cape Ann shore, we are still a league away. You must have patience."

"I can't wait to land," she said, smiling that their characters should be thus reversed, she chafing at delay and he counselling patience.

"See," he said, pointing to the *Arbella*, "they're manning their skiff. They mean to waft us in, though being so much larger they must wait themselves for high water and a fair wind."

At five o'clock of the soft June afternoon the *Jewell* reached Naumkeag at last, and dropped anchor in the south harbour. The low wooded shore dotted with people waving, and the huzzahs came now from their throats, not from those on the ship. These pressed together silently, gazing at journey's end. Master Wenn raised his voice in a prayer of thanksgiving, and Phebe, caught like the rest of them by the solemnity of the moment, bowed her head while the tears started to her eyes.

Mark was busy helping to lower the long-boat, and she was in the first load to leave the *Jewell*. As he lifted her down from the ladder, she was astonished to feel a sharp nostalgia. The battered little ship which she had so much detested was now friend and home. She looked back at it with misted eyes, and the faces of those still on board, even that of Mrs. Bagby, seemed transfigured and lovable.

But it was good to set foot on the land, though it seemed to sway and heave beneath her like the ship's deck. Delicious to refresh the eyes with the brown of earth and the brilliant green of the trees, loftier than any at home.

A score of men and three or four women had gathered at the landing-place to greet them, but they held back in respect for the two ministers. Mr. Higginson and Mr. Skelton, tall and solemn in their flowing black prunella robes, bowed to each arrival saying, "Welcome to Salem." It seemed that the Indian name "Naumkeag" had been replaced by the Hebrew word for "Peace."

Phebe held back a little, shy of these strange faces, and waiting for Mark to discover what was expected of them, and as she watched her joyous excitement dwindled. They looked haggard and ill, these people

...ho had already been settled for a year in the land of promise. Mr. Higginson, though only forty-six, seemed like an old man. She noted the trembling of his hands, the eyes sunk back into the sockets, the unwholesome red on his cheek-bones. Nor did his fellow minister, Mr. Skelton, look much stronger. They were all thin, ill-clothed and hollow-eyed, these men and women of Salem, and after the first cheer they fell silent, drawing together on the bank and watching with sombre looks while boat-loads of passengers disembarked from the Jewell.

"Come," said Mark, returning to Phebe, "we go to Governor Endicott's." They and the others moved along behind the ministers up a trampled path.

Phebe stared around her curiously, noted some rough earth dugouts roofed with bark, and tiny log huts beneath the trees, and thought with a thrill that these must be Indian dwellings. "I wonder how far it is to town?" she said to Mark. But Mr. Higginson overheard her, and to her mortification stopped and turned, looking down at her. "This is the town, mistress . . ." he said; his burning eyes showed reproof and a faint amusement. "This is the Highway," he pointed down the path, "and these our houses." His long thin hand pointed to the bark dugouts.

"Oh, to be sure, sir," she stammered, turning scarlet. The minister nodded and continued to walk. Phebe followed silently, striving against dismay. On her father's land these dwellings would not have been thought fit to house the swine.

They came to a clearing of uneven grassy ground, and near this clearing there were three wooden houses. The largest was two stories high and fairly built with windows and gables, almost like those at home. It was the Governor's house.

John Endicott met them on his stone doorstep and spoke a few gruff words of welcome, but he seemed out of temper, a sharp frown between his bushy brows, his pointed beard waggled irritably. For he was Governor no longer, as he had yesterday discovered upon the arrival of the Arbella, with the royal charter, and his successor, John Winthrop.

"You'd best return to your ship," he said, "till your new Governor lands and can regulate your proceedings. We've little food or shelter for you now, and there is much sickness."

Even Mark's enthusiasm was quenched by this, and after further consultation between Endicott, the ministers and the Jewell's master, the new arrivals trailed disconsolately back to the ship. So Phebe and Mark slept again in the cramped cabin they had foolishly thought to have seen the last of.

The first day on shore was filled with a feverish activity. When the Arbella had been warped up to the town dock near the Jewell, the great folk on board, the new Governor, the Saltonstalls, the Phillipses, all moved majestically down the gangplank ahead of its lesser passengers. Phebe watched eagerly for the Lady Arbella, until she landed last of all, walking slowly, her tall figure swathed in the fur-lined cloak, though

34

the day was warm. She was leaning on the arm of a tall, fair young man who was her husband, Mr. Isaac Johnson.

Phebe drew back shyly as the lady passed, but Arbella noticed her, and smiled with great sweetness. "Why, it's Mistress Honeywood, Isaac; I told you of her." She held out her hand. "How was the journey, my dear?"

Phebe took the thin white hand and curtsied. "I thought it would never end, milady. But now I scarce remember it, there's so much to do here."

Arbella nodded. Her blue eyes wandered past Phebe to the dusty lane which disappeared amongst the trees by the first earthen dugout. " 'Tis good to be on land," she said vaguely. "I'll soon gain strength again." This was to her husband, and Phebe saw the quick anxiety in his eyes.

"To be sure you will." He clasped the hand which rested on his arm. "Do you know where we're to go?" he asked of Phebe. "Governor Winthrop was to return for us, but he must have been detained."

"Oh yes, sir; they've prepared a fair wood house for you, down by the green; 'twas built last year by some gentleman of Mr. Higginson's party. At least," she added, her lips indenting with a rueful humour, "it's a fair enough house for Salem."

Isaac nodded, and she thought how much alike those two were, both tall and fine-drawn, both informed with an idealistic courage.

"We don't look for a castle in the wilderness," he said. "Will you guide us, mistress?"

Phebe gladly complied, but as she trudged up the path ahead of them her heart was troubled. They did not expect a castle, but did they expect the hardship and the actual hunger which already Phebe had discovered in Salem. This morning, when filling a pot with water for the cleansing of their garments, she had talked with a gaunt middle-aged woman near the spring. Goodwife Allen acted half crazed as she told of the previous winter; the wolves, the savages, the bitter bitter cold, the hunger and the sickness and fear. Her high thin voice whined through her drawn lips as though against its will. She had no pity, nor desire to frighten either. It seemed she could not stop from touching again and again, like a festering tooth, the horror of her memories. And Phebe could not get away, for the woman followed her about until another woman came and spoke sharply.

"Hold your tongue, Goody. 'Tis cruel to so frighten the young mistress here." And turning to Phebe she spoke lower. "Her two babes died this winter. She returns to England when the fleet goes—and so do I."

Home to England! Phebe had clamped her mind down hard against the great leap of longing and envy she had felt, and hope too. Surely Mark would soon see how different all was from his expectation.

Yet now, watching the Lady Arbella and her husband, she felt some shame for her own faint heart. *They* would never falter, thought Phebe proudly, nor turn back home in fear and failure.

Governor Winthrop came hurrying across the green to meet them, and Phebe, curtsying and drawing aside, noted the lady's gracious words, how she praised the beauty of the countryside, and even praised the compactness of the rough-planked two-room house which had been prepared for her.

The Governor and Mr. Johnson plunged at once into frowning consultation, and Phebe, warm from Arbella's smile of thanks, slipped away, back down the lane to the South River. A hundred yards up the slope from the landing place, near to the burial point—Mark had found them a shelter. He had bought it for a barrel of meal from one of the men who wished to leave Salem. It was twelve feet long and eight wide, made from a sapling frame, the walls and roof were of woven rushes and pine bark. Its floor was the ground, its door a single batten of hewn oak planks, and its end fireplace of piled field stones cemented with fishshell lime provided the only daylight through its wide square chimney.

It had been copied, like its fellows, from an Indian wigwam. It was dark and damp and smoky, but it was shelter.

Aye—but how will it be alone here—she thought, entering the wigwam to start their supper preparations, and the new trouble which the sight of Arbella had momentarily banished came back to plague her. For Mark was leaving her to sail southward with Governor Winthrop and most of the company and search for better lands.

At no time had Winthrop considered permanent settlement of his company in Salem, but he had found physical conditions far worse than he expected, nor were spiritual matters to his liking. The ministers, Higginson and Skelton, had unaccountably changed during their year here. They had come over as Puritans, averring their loyalty to the Mother Church and interested only in freeing her from certain forms of Papist corruption.

Had not Mr. Higginson upon taking the last sight of England a year ago cried, "Farewell, the Church of God in England and all the Christian friends there. We do not go to New England as Separatists from the Church of England—but we go to practise the positive part of Church reformation, and propagate the gospel in America."

And yet upon arrival in Salem, Winthrop found that these same ministers had adopted the congregational polity and affiliated themselves with the Separatist Church at Plymouth. And so strict in conscience had they become that Winthrop's company, being no members of the Salem Church, were not even invited to worship with them on the Lord's Day.

There were, besides, many jealousies; the earlier settlers under Endicott, and the ministers felt themselves dispossessed by new authority, just as Roger Conant and his settlers had been literally dispossessed, in 1628, by the arrival of Endicott.

So Winthrop would sail again tomorrow on the *Arbella* to explore Massachusetts Bay and decide on a more welcoming site for the new settlement. Most of the male passengers would accompany him, and Mark too, of course, already impatient with Salem, but ever hopeful and eager for more adventuring.

I must be reasonable, thought Phebe, sighing. I can manage alone for a time. She moved around the wigwam, trying to make it more homelike. Though all the *Jewell's* freight had not yet been unloaded, the Honeywoods had found some of their household gear, and together carried it to the wigwam. There were blankets to sleep on, the two chests of clothing, a skillet and spoon, and an iron pot which Phebe, feeling very housewifely, hung from the green lug pole left by the earlier tenant. And there were the andirons. They gave an incongruous and elegant air to the rough Indian fireplace, and Mark had been impatient with her insistence that they must be used. But when their first fire blazed and they sat down on the blankets to eat, he admitted that they were sturdy, well-made dogs, and did better than the stones the other new settlers were using.

They supped that night on pease-porridge and a large catfish which Mark had caught in the river. And they had beer, bought with one of the precious shillings from a sailor on the *Arbella*. But the shillings were not so precious here, Phebe had soon realized; only to those who were returning to England. Here nothing mattered but food.

It had not occurred to Mark that she might be short of food during his absence, since they had brought barrels of pickled meat, flour, and pease, but already Phebe had seen enough of the conditions to realize the vital importance of conserving supplies as long as possible—in case they stayed long. Always that reservation whispered in her heart.

But there were wild strawberries in the woods, and mussels and clams at low tide for the picking.

"You'll not be frightened to be alone, Phebe?" said Mark suddenly, seeing her pensive. "I'll be back soon. You know how little I wish to leave you—but I must."

"I know, dear," she said gently, for she saw that he was shaken from the bustle of novelty and action which had made him thoughtless, and that there was anxious awareness of her in his eyes. "No, I won't be frightened. Why, I can see the ship from our doorway, and then there are all the other folk—so near."

"The Lady Arbella," he said with a curt laugh. "I vow you dote upon her noble ladyship. I never thought to find you so fawning. God's blood, Phebe—it's to be rid of such as her I quitted England!"

She had been sitting beside him on the bed-roll, and now she rose and walked away from him to the doorway. "It has nothing to do with her rank, Mark." She spoke with a coldness and dignity.

"What is it, then?" he asked in a quieter tone, standing up beside her.

She could not answer. Never had she found it easy to speak of the secret things in her heart. The Lady Arbella was like a shining silken banner for the humble heart to follow. She was beauty, she was courage, and she was England, here on this alien and unfriendly soil. Mark would never understand that, nor need to. He needed no symbol to strengthen him.

She shook her head. "I cannot say."

But Mark was no longer attending, he had forgotten his question in watching the curve of her rosy cheek and the roundness of her neck and bosom. He picked her up and sat down with her on his knee, where he held her fast, pulled off her cap and tossed it in the corner, rumpled and loosened her smooth brown hair.

"Not so solemn, sweetheart," he whispered. "We must be merry in our fine new home."

She resisted at first, being still grieved by their difference. But he began to caress her playfully, teasing her with mock anger, kissing away her protests until at last he had her laughing, too, and as eagerly amorous as he.

The *Arbella* and Governor Winthrop came back in a few days, he having decided to gather up his company and establish a temporary settlement in Charlestown. It was not an ideal site, since the peninsula was small and the water supply very scanty, but it would serve as a base for further exploration.

Phebe had been bitterly disappointed that Mark had not also returned to Salem. He had, however, sent her a letter which was delivered to her wigwam by a friendly sailor.

She carried the letter inside her dwelling, and stared at it with a mixture of apprehension, embarrassment and pride. Mark knew—or had he forgotten—that she could not read; that was an accomplishment deemed useless to a yeoman's daughter. She turned the half sheet of folded paper, admiring the red seal stamped with a small signet, and guessed, accurately, that he, never backward in fulfilling his impulses, had borrowed all from one of the great folk on board.

At last she broke the seal and stared at the lines of cramped and blotted writing.

"Swete wife be not vext I linger too finde us setlment. Ther is muche to see but the peple are not so as we ded expect. Ther is good stor of feishe but harde to come bye and not enuf provisseyenes.

"Bee stout harted.

"Thy lovinge husband
M. Hunywood."

She followed each word with her finger, her brows drawn together. Almost she got the sense of it, but she was not sure. A certainty born of her love for him told her that here was no particular bad news, and that he had written the letter so that she might have an immediate token of him, and for this she bent her head and kissed the paper. But it was exasperating not to know precisely the meaning.

She considered awhile, then nodded her head with decision. There was but one person in Salem who could read the letter, yet who would not smile at it or Phebe's ignorance; one person to whose own delicacy of understanding one would not shrink from exposing intimacy.

Phebe took the hearth shovel, dug into the earth in the corner of the wigwam and pulled from its hiding-place the key of her bride chest. This and Mark's oaken chest stood in the wigwam with the precious provisions.

She drew out her best dress, a soft crimson gown with slashed sleeves, made of a silk and wool fabric newly fashionable in England, called Farandine. She put on her wedding ruff and cuffs made of cobweb lawn trimmed with Mechlin lace, and she rejoiced that the day being so mild, she might dispense with the heavy, hooded serge cloak which had done hard duty on the ship and was her only outer garment. Before donning her best lace-trimmed cap, she pulled her soft brown hair forward into loose ringlets about her ears, and examined the effects in a small steel looking-glass.

Then she set forth up the road towards the common, happy in the feminine consciousness of being suitably dressed for her visit. Not so elegant as to affront the gentry, nor in coarse sad-coloured clothes like the goodwives and maidservants.

The weather was very hot, warmer than it ever was in England, and the lane was dusty. Soon she came to the village "green," no green now, but a square of trodden earth and brownish stubble. Some women clustered as usual around the well, gossiping while they drew water for their households. At the other end near the stocks—unoccupied today—three young men played at stool-ball, ceasing frequently for thirst-quenching at the Ordinary near by. Idleness like this was naturally frowned upon by the magistrates, but the return of the *Arbella* and Governor Winthrop's intent to remove all his settlers on the morrow had relaxed supervision.

Phebe continued past the two-room houses belonging to Mr. Higginson and Mr. Skelton, past the Governor's larger frame house, where there was much bustle of coming and going, for Winthrop was inside and holding conference, and on a little way up the lane to the next house, which was that of the Lady Arbella.

She knocked timidly and waited. There was a scuffle within and suppressed giggles. At last the door was opened by a frowsy maid, her cap awry, her holland apron stained with the claret she had evidently been sampling. She stared sullenly at Phebe, impudence just held in check by Phebe's clothing and dignity.

"Might I have a word with the Lady Arbella, if it's convenient?" said Phebe.

"'Er Ladyship's resting," answered the girl in her flat Lincolnshire twang; "she wants no company." And she made to shut the door, staying her hand at the sound of a clear firm voice calling, "Who's at the door, Molly?"

"Mistress Honeywood," supplied Phebe. The maid shrugged and, walking two steps to the shut door on the right, imparted this information.

"Let her enter," called Arbella. Molly stood sulkily aside long enough for Phebe to pass, then darted back to the house's other room, the hall or kitchen, where she rejoined her two companions by the wine cask.

Phebe entered the other room, which was also the bedchamber. The servants slept above the kitchen in the unfinished loft.

Arbella lay on a feather bed raised a foot from the planks by a rough pine frame. She wore only a bedrobe of transparent blue tiffany, but her pale face was bedewed. Her golden hair as it branched from her forehead was dark with sweat, and there were bistre shadows beneath the large blue eyes. But her smile as she greeted Phebe had its usual gallant sweetness.

"Welcome, mistress; it's kind that you come to visit me. How comely you look."

"To do you honour, milady," said Phebe, accepting the ladder-back chair indicated by Arbella. " 'Tis most good of you to receive me."

Arbella shook her head. "Nay, I'm much alone. My husband still at Charlestown, and my friends who returned, the Governor and Sir Richard, so much occupied. And my servants . . ." She shook her head again. "But you saw Molly, how she was. And the other's worse. It's hard to believe a new country or a sea voyage could so change them. And I've not—not yet— the strength to rule them properly. I must save my strength."

As she said this, a light came into her eyes and her lips lifted in a joyous and secret smile. She looked at Phebe and saw in the younger woman's face the eager admiration which had been there from their first meeting in Yarmouth, and the need to speak overcame Arbella's reticence.

"I'm with child," she said very low. "At last. Wed seven years, and I had lost all hope. Our dear Lord has rewarded me for braving the new land."

Phebe swallowed. For an instant she could not properly answer the lady's confidence. It pierced through the foolish barrier Phebe had built against her own realization. And through the rent, like the mounting sound of tempest waves, she heard the rushing of fear.

And again Arbella had shamed her, by the radiance in her thin face and the thrill in the low voice.

"I'm happy for you, milady," Phebe said gently. She hesitated. "I think I too am with child."

Arbella gave a little cry and stretched out her hand until Phebe came to the bedside and took it in hers. "We have then that great bond between us," said Arbella. Her pale cheeks flushed, and she sat up, her long braids of wheat-coloured hair falling back across her thin shoulders. "Tell me . . ." And she asked eager questions, and as they talked together she seemed the younger of the two women.

Both babies would be born in the winter, they decided: Arbella's the earlier, in January, for she had reason to guess it had been conceived in England before the sailing. "And you will stay near me, Phebe—won't you," Arbella said, "that our babies may know each other and grow together in the new land?"

"Indeed I hope so, milady." Now Phebe's eyes too were shining; Arbella's courage and Arbella's pride had become hers too. "But I don't know where Mark will decide our settlement. He—wrote me a letter, I brought it . . ." Phebe stopped and blushed. "I hoped . . ." She stared down at the letter in her hand.

Arbella was briefly puzzled. She had been talking to this girl as she would have talked to her own sister, Lady Susan, and had forgotten that there was difference between them. Nor did the rigid class distinction seem to matter much in the wilderness. She covered Phebe's embarrassment at once by taking the letter and calmly reading it aloud.

" 'Tis evident he takes thought of you and loves you," she commented, smiling.

Phebe smiled back shyly, unable to suppress the leap of hope again. If Mark continued to be disappointed in conditions as he found them—perhaps after a few months of roving and striving . . .

"I too had a letter this morning from my husband," said Arbella. "He favours a place called Shawmut. It's across a river from Charlestown, and he is starting to prepare for me. You must bear on your Mark to settle there, too."

Phebe was silent for a moment, glad that the lady did not guess her unbecoming hope and considering this new idea.

"Why, is there fish at this Shawmut, your ladyship?" she asked with her sudden quiet twinkle.

Arbella laughed. "There must be. Is he still set on fishing."

"More than ever. He is most apt." But he might fish from Weymouth at home, she thought, it was scarcely farther to the great fishing banks from there than it was from any part of this unwelcoming wilderness.

"I shall speak to Mr. Johnson," said Arbella decisively. She said nothing more, but she was thinking. She would use her influence to settle the Honeywoods in Shawmut, or Boston as Isaac proposed to call it from their own shire town.

"When the Governor leaves again," she said with decision, "he'll bear a letter to my husband. I shall request that he find your Mark and take interest in him."

Phebe gratefully acquiesced, nor voiced her doubt of Mark's reception of this affectionate and natural patronage.

That was the first of many visits. As the days passed and the heat-wave lessened, Arbella grew stronger, and together Phebe and she stood on the bank by the landing-place and watched the ship *Arbella* sail down the river, bound southward to the new plantations with 200 aboard her.

Except for the few like Phebe and Arbella who remained to wait for their men to fetch them, and the very few who desired to settle here, Salem reverted to its earlier population. In the North Village there lived a handful of the earliest planters who had not followed Roger Conant across the river to Beverley; in the South or Main Village lived those who still survived from the companies which had come with Endicott or the two ministers. True, throughout June and July many ships touched at Salem, as the rest of Winthrop's fleet straggled into port. But the passengers were not disembarked. All sailed again at once for Charlestown to join the others.

On July 3rd, Phebe, asleep in her wigwam, heard the now familiar shouts and creakings and bustle which meant the arrival of another ship. She dressed hastily and, opening her door, was delighted to see that it was the *Hopewell*, which had in England been destined for freight. Moorings and cacklings and bleatings echoed in the early morning air, and the inhabitants of Salem, crowding down to the dock, let out a cheer. Most of them were disappointed. The live-stock must go on to Charlestown, where already there was famine. But Phebe, finding courage to board and seek out the master herself, discovered that her milch-cow had survived the trip, and demanded that it be landed.

In this she would not have succeeded, between the captain's haste to be on to Charlestown and finish this tedious trip, and her lack of the necessary papers, had not Arbella, hastily summoned by Phebe, come down to the boat and straightened the matter.

Phebe coaxed and tugged the terrified cow down the gangplank; and when her prize was safely on shore could not resist kissing the soft fawn-coloured muzzle. Betsy was a living link with home. Phebe had last seen her standing in Edmunds's barn, her new calf beside her and placidly munching while the younger children decorated her with a wreath of early primroses—"Because Betsy was a cow princess and going to America with sister Phebe."

Phebe soothed the cow with soft whispers: "Soooo, Betsy—hush, Betsy; it's on land again you are. Ah, poor beast, you're nearly dry. Didn't they milk you right or was it the seasickness?"

The cow looked at her mournfully, and Phebe threw her arm around the warm furry neck.

The Lady Arbella had been watching curiously and with some amusement. "Aren't you afraid of its horns?" she asked. "I've never seen a cow so close before."

Phebe looked quickly from the cow to her friend. Friend, yes, the only one in Salem, and they seemed to share much together. But in truth they did not. The lady's fine white hands had never laboured with anything rougher than an embroidery needle. A spasm of homesickness overpowered Phebe—for her father's hearty laugh and broad speech, for her mother's kindly bustle. "Phebe child, do you finish the milking, the dairymaids are at the churns." For the fresh voices of the younger children singing, "Oh, lavender's green, dilly, dilly"; and tumbling about the grassy courtyard, while the doves cooed accompaniment from their cote.

"I've milked Betsy many times, milady," she said very low, and pulling on the halter, she began to lead the cow up the path from the dock to her wigwam.

Arbella followed. "Will the animal not be a great care?" she asked gently. "And how will you feed it?"

Phebe considered. "I'll arrange with little Benjy, the herd, to take her each day to the common to graze, with the other stock. At night I can tether her by my door. 'Twill be well worth it, if I can coax her milk back."

"For butter?"

Phebe nodded. "If I can borrow a churn, but mostly to drink. Milk will do us good. You, too, milady."

Arbella looked so astonished that Phebe smiled. She knew that except on farms neither milk nor plain water was considered wholesome. Arbella, like all the gentry, drank wines, often diluted. The lower classes drank strong liquor, beer or cider or mead. But milk was considered valuable only for its ability to produce cheese and butter.

Nor did she ever persuade Arbella to try it. By the time the cow had adjusted herself to her new home and the coarse pasture land on the common so that Phebe's persuasive handling would fill a night and morning pail, Arbella was confined to her bed again with a mysterious illness. And the *Arbella's* physician, Mr. Gager, was in attendance.

Those were grim days that set in after the middle of July. Many were sick besides the Lady Arbella, some with the ship-fever which swelled mouths, loosened teeth and sent cruel pains through the body. Others, like the Lady herself, were afflicted by excessive languor, headache and colic, and, though often able to get about, seemed to grow burning hot towards evening, and day by day to lose strength. The weather too ceased to be pleasant. There was much heavy rain. The lanes turned to quagmires. The reed thatching on Phebe's wigwam leaked in a dozen places, and when there was no rain, the mosquitoes swarmed through the new-made crannies and attacked voraciously. Phebe set her teeth and settled to day-to-day endurance as she had on the boat. The friendly Naumkeag Indians came and went in town. She had quickly become accustomed to their nakedness and dark, painted faces, and she learned to barter with them, as did the others. A little of her meal she had exchanged for corn and pompions, the great golden fruit which might be baked or stewed into good food.

Sometimes she dug clams or made a hasty pudding from the corn; but mostly she lived on corn cakes baked on a shovel over the flames — and Betsy's milk. She grew thin and sometimes felt light headed, and that the wigwam and the rain and the mosquitoes, the heavy-eyed people in the village, the close-pressing forest — and even Arbella lying white and silent in her house — were all painted on smoke. Shifting figures without reality that a strong breath might blow away. Still she had few pains. She even found a way of lessening the surface discomfort from the mosquitoes. On the lane to the Common she had spied a small herb, pennyroyal, much like that which grew at home. Well instructed by her mother in the making of simples, she had gathered a horde of it, and distilled it over boiling water. The pungent mint odour when rubbed on the skin repelled fleas at home, and did discourage the mosquitoes here.

She carried some of it to Lady Arbella on one of her daily visits. There was now no need to knock. Molly, the impudent maidservant, was herself ill and lay groaning in the loft. The manservant and the other maid gave only grudging and frightened service, held from actual escape by the knowledge that there was no safe place to go.

Phebe's daily arrival was heartily welcomed, for she did much of the nursing.

Today Mr. Gager, the physician, was there, bleeding Arbella. He acknowledged Phebe's quiet entrance by a curt nod, and went on with his task. Phebe took off her muddy shoes and, placing them in a corner of the room, came to the foot of the bed. Arbella started to smile a greeting as she always did, but at once her gaze slid past Phebe, and

43

into the staring blue eyes came a distant, intent look. "Think you, madam, 'twill be a fine day for the chase?" she said. "I hear the huntsman winding their horns. Will Charles ride the grey stallion?"

Phebe's breath caught, and her eyes met the physician's. His mouth set, and he nodded his grey head. "She wanders." He sighed. "It's enteric, I believe. There are the rose spots." He drew the coverlet down a little. The delicate white skin of the swelling abdomen and slender waist was sprinkled with pinkish dots.

"I must find someone to help you and the servants," he said, rising. "But so many are sick. Each day a new case. Would that her husband were back," he added half to himself.

"I'm not leaving her," said Phebe.

William Gager picked up his leech-bag and threw in the lancet. "You're a good girl, mistress. I'll come back later. I—I must rest. Give her nothing but wine and this oil of fennel." He indicated a flask on the rough stool by the bedside. He put his hand to his head, and swayed a little as he stood up. Phebe saw his lips twitch and fear pull at his face. "This thrice-cursed country," he said under his breath, and went out.

Phebe went to the kitchen for a pewter basin. The little maid sat on a stool, listlessly turning two spitted rabbits above the flames. The manservant had gone to the forest for firewood. Above in the loft the sick maid, Molly, whimpered incessantly. Phebe climbed the ladder, and did what she could to bring comfort, changing the fouled linen, holding the mug of claret while the girl drank. Then she hurried back to the sicker patient with a basin of rain water, washed Arbella's thin fair body, then rubbed it gently with the pennyroyal. Despite the tight-shut windows mosquitoes whined in the dark little room and the rain beat without ceasing on the roof.

Arbella was still wandering. Sometimes she thought herself a child in Tattershall Castle or riding through Sherwood Forest. Sometimes she relived her bridal day, and spoke to Isaac, her husband, with such poignancy and passion that Phebe flushed and murmured, "Oh hush, my dear Lady, hush."

Worst of all, as the long grey day wore on, Arbella began to talk of her child, thinking that it had been born, and demanding of Phebe that she bring it to her. "I wish my son," she said imperiously. "All in this new land rejoice that he is born. Why don't you rejoice? How dare you look so sad, wench! Bring me my son."

Phebe soothed her tenderly, replacing the cool cloth on the burning forehead, stroking the restless hands that plucked at the coverlet.

At dusk Arbella became quieter, it seemed the fever eased. She lay still a long time, her eyes closed, her hand clinging to Phebe's. Then the blue eyes opened and gazed at the girl with full recognition. "You must rest, dear," she whispered. "You do too much for me. You must think of your babe."

Phebe shook her head, smiling. "No, I'm strong. Nursing is nothing to me. I've done it often at home."

Her last unconsidered word seemed to crash through the room, like the first toll of a passing bell. A spasm twisted Arbella's face, while the word went echoing and swelling around them.

Blundering fool, cried Phebe to herself, and she spoke again with cheerful resolution. "Here now is home, milady, and soon 'twill feel so." She rose briskly, to smooth the bedding.

Arbella stopped her. "Do you remember, Phebe, Mr. Higginson's sermon on the Sabbath? 'What went ye out into the wilderness to see? A reed shaken with the wind?' We must not hark back. Promise me, Phebe"—she rose painfully on her elbow, her eyes beseeching—"promise me, you'll not give up—no matter what may happen."

Phebe tried to speak, to give easy assurance, but she could not. Mr. Higginson had died the day before. Arbella did not know that. There was death in every dwelling—and hunger and despair. When Mark came, tired perhaps of the new adventure, restless again, and wishing to go home—home—home—home. The forbidden, the exquisite music.

Arbella sank back on to the pillow, the light faded from her eyes. "I had no right to ask you that, child. Your future is in God's hands—as is mine." She drew a shaking sigh, that ended in a sudden cry of pain. The brief interval of peace was ended. The pain and noises in her head returned and the cruel gripings in her distended belly. Phebe almost welcomed the mounting fever, for it gave surcease from the pain as Arbella's mind escaped again, back—now always back into the tranquil, the sheltered, days of her childhood.

All the interminable night Phebe watched beside Arbella, refusing the little maid's reluctant offer to help. "You look after Molly," she told the girl, "and keep the fire up for hot water. I'll look to her ladyship."

Once in the evening a neighbour, Mistress Horne, hurried in, saying that Mr. Gager the physician had told her how very ill the Lady Arbella was. Mr. Gager himself was suffering with headache and vomiting so that he could not rise from bed.

Phebe thanked her, but said that she could manage alone. Mistress Horne's kind, worried face showed relief. "I'm glad to hear it, my dear, for I've heavy duties at home, my little girl puking blood and my youngest most feverish. You've none but yourself to consider, have you, mistress?"

Phebe shook her head. The two women stood by Arbella's bedside together. Mrs. Horne made a sound in her throat, and whispered, "Dear—she do look bad. Such a sweet woman. I was watching from my window the day she landed and come walking down the street with her fine young husband. She looked so kindly and so fair. But I feared then 'twould take rougher clay than she is to stand the roughness here."

"She'll get well," said Phebe sharply. "Many do have the burning fever and get well."

Mrs. Horne sighed and turned from the bed. "We can hope so. But many do not." She walked to the wall and peered curiously into Arbella's looking-glass. "What a frump I've grown," she said, pushing distractedly at the lank hair around her perspiring face. Then seeing

Phebe's expression, she said, "I'm not unfeeling, my dear, but one gets used to death here. Needs must or go mad." She straightened her linen cap, gave a tug to her collar. "They say there's a ship sighted way off down the bay. If it's another from England, I hope they bring us provisions as well as more mouths to eat 'em."

"But maybe," cried Phebe, "it's from Charlestown—from the Governor—maybe it's her husband at last." She looked towards the bed. "And mine," she added very low.

"Mayhap it is," said the woman kindly and without the slightest conviction. "Pray on't." she advised, opening the door. "Miracles are wrought by prayer."

Through the night Phebe thought of this. They did live by prayer here, and they did seem to have special understanding and closeness to God. At home God stayed in church. He lived in the candles and the incense and the golden cross, in the voices of the choir boys, in the slow, solemn movements of the lace-frocked priest. But she had never thought to find Him elsewhere.

She tried to pray, but no words came, nor could she remember the words of the prayer-book. Neither could she believe that any prayer might change the identity of that ship in the bay. The prayer, therefore, which came to her heart but could find no utterance was for Lady Arbella. And she made a foolish covenant. If the lady recovered it would be easy to join her Church, for had they not in a dozen conversations agreed to stay near each other and Phebe to follow her in all things.

In the first rose light of the new summer day, she heard the sound of running feet on the road outside. She darted to the door and flung it open. She saw five men crowding upon the threshold, and she gave a cry to the man in front. "Oh, Mr. Johnson, thank God." The blond young man gave her a frightened look and pushed past her as she clung to the door frame. She saw the curly head behind and higher than the others, she tried to speak again, but a rocking giddiness swept through her head. The sunlit road billowed and darkened. She felt strong arms seize her as she slipped down to the ground.

She opened her eyes to the familiar ragged thatching of the wigwam. Her bemused gaze wandered from a chink between the reeds and the slit of blue sky it revealed to Mark's frightened face bending close to her own. He knelt beside her on their mattress, and his arms still supported her. She gave a little sigh of content and, turning her head, nuzzled for her accustomed place on his shoulder.

"Sweetheart!" he cried sharply, feeling her body relax against him and seeing her lids droop, "don't swoon again. Phebe, are you ill?"

He almost shook her in his anxiety. She raised her head and kissed him on the mouth. "Not ill," she said drowsily. "Hungry, and so glad you're back."

His frown cleared. Always and so easily she could reassure him. He smiled and kissed her hard and long. She submitted contentedly, willing enough to drift with him to that moment which ensured forgetfulness of all else.

But Mark had been alarmed when she slid off Lady Arbella's stone step into his arms, and he saw now how pale and thin she was. He shook his head and put her from him. "Food first, poppet," he said, standing up. "I've no wish to bed a wraith. You lie there, I'll do all."

He had brought a venison steak, gift as he explained of a Mr. Isaac Allerton, of whom he had seen much and in whom he had great interest. She watched him with some surprise as he hacked off slices with his hunting knife and dexterously broiled them over the fire. He had learned much apparently in those weeks he had been away. Never before had he had anything to do with cookery.

He fed her the rich gamy meat, and brought her mugs of beer until she could hold no more, and she sighed deeply and loosened her belt to enjoy the delicious fullness.

Mark chuckled, glad to see the colour come back to her cheeks, and amused that she who was always so fastidious should loosen her clothing. But as he gazed at her a new look crossed his face.

"Phebe," he said, half teasing, half startled, "did the venison fill you so much, or can it be—aren't you more full-bellied?"

Phebe looked down at her gown. "You have sharp eyes, love," she said quietly. "I had not thought to show yet." She spoke so quietly, because still the old fear leaped at her, and now the new fear too, the fear for Arbella, which her exhaustion had put aside for this past hour.

Mark, puzzled by her voice and uncertain as all young husbands, persisted, "You mean, I've got you with child? . . ."

At this, despite her fears, she could not help laughing. "Oh, Mark, you great goose. Who else? Nor should it surprise you; you're lusty enough, the Lord knows."

She saw him adjusting himself to this new idea. He bent and kissed her cheek, carefully, as though she were of a sudden turned to crystal. Then his natural exuberance returned and he gave a great roar of mirth. "You had better not let any of those mewling Separatists hear you call on the Lord to witness lustiness! They'd sew a letter 'L' to your bodice for lewd, and very like add a 'B' for blasphemy. Pah!" he cried, scowling. "They're a narrow canting lot. I've no stomach for all this godly talk and conscience searching. Nor was it what we were led to expect when we came. Why else did Master White get 'em to sign 'The Humble Request' on the *Arbella* back at Yarmouth except to show we would not separate. Promised we were we'd be let alone in our own beliefs. Now Winthrop's getting sour as the rest of them."

"They're not all so bad, Mark," Phebe said softly. But he scowled even harder, staring at the earthen floor.

"You've no say in running a town unless you're a freeman; you can't be a freeman unless you join the Church; you can't join the Church without the minister permits. I'll never make churchman, and I've seen no minister I like here yet. 'Tis cramping in its own way as the Old Country."

Phebe drew in her breath. "Then what will you do, Mark," she asked, watching him very close, "if you've found no place to your liking for our settlement?"

He raised his head and looked at her. "Aye, but I think I have."

Her heart slowed and her mouth grew dry. "Tell me then—no, tell me first about your journey, from the beginning."

For she dreaded to hear of any decision, and well knew how much harder it would be to change his mind after he had voiced it.

He nodded, for he was himself unsure as yet, and glad to clear his mind by talking. "Well, as you know, we set off from here with fair winds . . ."

He described the two-day voyage in somewhat more nautical detail than she could understand. They had passed something called Nahant, threaded their way amongst a great many little islands, entered the mouth of the Charles, and landed passengers at the ramshackle collection of tents and wigwams called Charlestown. The place appealed to nobody, it was cramped and barren, but it was necessary to stop somewhere while the leaders searched farther.

The minister, Mr. Phillips, set off to explore with Saltonstall up the Charles in search of a new site, the Governor went up the Mystic for the same purpose. Mark, however, had no intention of settling inland, and crossing the Charles by canoe, he had been among the first to explore the peninsula called Shawmut with its three rounded hills. They found a settler there, a taciturn, well-lettered man called Blackstone. He had lived there quite alone five years, and made himself most snug in a two-roomed cabin filled with books and surrounded by a small garden and three apple trees.

He was a man, said Mark, who made it clear he liked solitude, and he had been watching the activities across the river with considerable dismay. But he was also a gentleman, and his greeting was not uncordial.

The Lady Arbella's husband, Isaac Johnson, was much taken with the site, and when Governor Winthrop returned from the Mystic River, both men held long conferences with Mr. Blackstone, who unselfishly agreed that they might settle at Shawmut if they wished. He would stay awhile and help them, since he knew the secrets of the country, the best springs, the most fertile soil, and was also well-liked by the Indians. "But," said he gravely, all his speech was slow and grave, but in this instance his eyes twinkled a bit, "I'll soon be off to the wilderness, for I doubt not I'll grow as weary of the 'lord brethren' here as I did of the 'lord Bishops' in old England."

Mark had heard this speech and applauded it.

The town planning began at once. Shawmut was rechristened Boston, land was allotted, Master John Wilson was appointed minister, settlers poured in as the ships from England docked almost daily, and Mark found it not at all to his liking.

It was then that he met Isaac Allerton. There was a make-shift ordinary in a hut on the beach at Charlestown, and Mark had gone in one evening for a tankard of metheglin from a cask just arrived by the *Success*.

He had been tired and discouraged, but the strong fermented honey liquor put new life into him. Perhaps it also had something to do with his immediate interest in a man who entered the smoky little room, and also called for drink.

48

He was a man in his middle forties, rather short and comfortably plump. His round face was clean shaven, his full cheeks a healthy red, doubtless from the seafaring life, but Mark found it pleasant to see again a man who appeared well-fed and sanguine, the type of beef-eating country squire who seemed seldom to emigrate. The man was well dressed, too, in a slashed doublet of green serge lined with leather, glossy calamanco breeches, and a silver filigree buckle on his beaver hat.

They fell into conversation, and Mark was astonished to find that this Mr. Isaac Allerton was a Separatist from Plymouth, of importance to that colony, having been Assistant Governor for many years, negotiator of Colony business in London, and having recently taken as a second wife Fear Brewster, daughter of the Elder.

Mr. Allerton had been trading in Maine in his ship the *White Angel*. He had been twice to England in her, he had just stopped at Salem, but was returning to Plymouth with a cargo of stockings, tape, pins, and rugs, on which, though he did not say so, he expected to make a handsome profit. Nor did he say that he was becoming unpopular at Plymouth, where a growing disgust at the sharp increase in the colony's floating debt began to focus attention on the vague activities of their agent, Mr. Allerton. True he always had satisfactory explanations, and there was about him an ingenuousness that disarmed criticism, but even his father-in-law, Elder Brewster, was becoming aware that Isaac's successful trading expeditions always seemed to impoverish the colony.

Mark did, however, gather that Mr. Allerton, being somewhat wearied of life in Plymouth, intended to settle elsewhere. And that, having investigated many lines of commerce, he had decided on a new one which would certainly make his fortune—fishing.

"Here," said Mark, smiling at Phebe, "you may be sure I pricked my ears and questioned him narrowly." He paused, and she knew that now would come something of importance, by the offhand tone in his voice. "You know the point of land across the little harbour here."

"You mean that they call Derby Head?"

Often she had stood on the Salem wharf and gazed at the low headland across the water. For her as for the earlier Dorset people it aroused a poignant memory, being by some trick of nature shaped exactly like the headland at the mouth of the River Wey.

She brought her thoughts back, for Mark had gone on. "He told me he had land and a fishing-stage at the other side of Derby Fort. He calls the place Marblehead, and says it is the best harbour for fishing on the coast. He will remove there himself soon, and he says I may share in the venture with him."

"Is it there you mean to settle, then?" asked Phebe slowly. "But are there others there, Mark?"

"Oh, a fisherman or two, I believe. They do say a Guernsey wight named Dolliber wintered there last year in a hogshead." He chuckled as he saw her expression. "But when Mr. Allerton comes, it'll make all the difference. I go there with him tomorrow to look at the place."

"Is it far from here?" she asked presently, because Mark seemed waiting for her to speak.

"Not by water, an hour's sail with a fair breeze. Come, poppet—don't look so dismal. I vow it'll be the very place for us. I'll decide when I've seen it."

He got up, stretching his long legs and yawning. His black curls grazed the thatching, and under the worn red-leather doublet she saw the strength of his shoulders, the bulge of his arms. Yes, he was a proper man, and it was right that he should rule. But there was another love for which she felt allegiance; small indeed beside her love for Mark, but still an insistent claim, and she would have no peace until she spoke of it.

She watched him shamble about the wigwam, then pick up his fowling-piece. He settled on the stool, scooped up a handful of tinder, and, whistling through his teeth, fell to cleaning his gun.

Her heart beat fast as she rinsed the pewter beer mugs from a cask of rain-water outside the wigwam, burnished them to silver with a fair linen cloth as her mother had taught her, and placed them on top of her bride chest. She tended the fire and the hearth, sweeping the ashes neatly behind the great andirons with a twig besom she had made.

"Mark . . ."

He nodded, intent on the hammer of his fowling-piece.

"While you were gone, I've come close to the Lady Arbella . . ."

He clicked the hammer again, and his lips tightened. "So I supposed, since you swooned on her doorstep. It angers me to see you headstrong. You knew my wishes."

Phebe sighed and attacked obliquely. "But didn't you like Mr. Johnson? You saw much of him at the bay."

Mark shrugged. "He's well enough for one of the canting East County folk. He talks overmuch about the state of grace."

"If we should settle in Boston near them, I'm sure he'd find you preferment; you might be freeman at once. Nay wait, dear"—for he had shaken off her hand and his lower lip jutted out—"I ask only that you open your mind to the thought. True, they can help us advance, but you can also help them; they've need of a great strong man like you in the new plantation."

He made a derisive sound. "What cozzening is this, Phebe! You think I don't smell some womanish plot? You and your meddlesome peeress!"

Anger struck through her and she took a step back. But she looked at his stubborn side-turned face, at the fall of his hair which covered the sickening mutilation of his ear, and her anger died.

She came close again and spoke very soft. "Our babes will be born near the same time, Mark. Their interest would mean much. It's not us I think of, but of our child."

His hand fell from the fowling-piece, and he turned his head. "God blast it. I'd forgot the child." He reached out and pinched her cheek in unwilling contrition. "Poor lass—small wonder you seem so dithering."

He rose and walked to the doorway of the wigwam. The coming of a child was a problem he had not anticipated in his enthusiasm for Allerton's proposal. Nor had he till now thought of the danger for Phebe. It crossed his mind that he should have left her at home. Safe she would have been, comfortable—and no encumbrance until he had made permanent settlement. But he thought, too, of her softness and warmth. The full curving mouth that always spoke gently, and yet parted in sharp desire to his kiss.

"It may be the Marble harbour'll not suit me at all," he said carelessly. "Let's forget the matter for now."

He set sail with Isaac Allerton the next morning in the *White Angel* for Marblehead, and while he was gone one problem was settled.

The Lady Arbella died that evening in her husband's arms. There were many crowded into the small room, and Phebe huddled into the far corner by the door. Mr. Johnson himself had sent for her earlier, saying that the Lady called for her. Arbella had had one excruciatingly sharp pain, and then all pain had stopped. The fever red had left her thin cheeks, and they became yellow-white as the sheet on which she lay. Master Gager, the physician, himself very ill, had been carried to her bedside and carried away again. He had recognized the symptom which he hourly expected in himself. The intestine had been perforated and there was no hope.

Almost at once the delirium left Arbella, and she knew what was going to happen. Before she sank into a stupor, she greeted Phebe with the old sweet smile. "So we cannot plan for our babes together, since God has other plans for me and mine. Nay, don't weep, Phebe, I am content to obey His will; there is no other happiness, child."

This Phebe, filled with grief and rebellion, could not believe. She tried to pray when the others did. Isaac Johnson, though himself distracted with sorrow, could pray; and Master Skelton, the minister, and Master Endicott, and the hushed neighbours who stood by the entry and on the steps. But Phebe could not. She envied them their certainty of being able to pierce the iron wall of death, windowing it with blue glimpses and a consoling light beyond, but Phebe, helping to shroud the body of her dearly loved friend, could find no comfort.

The Lady Arbella was laid near Master Higginson on the Burial Point that jutted close to the South River. And atop the grave they placed a heavy flat field stone—for fear of wolves. Phebe, standing apart from the others, watched the hasty ceremony with a misery so bitter that it was near to disgust. Everywhere on the Point there were new mounds, even now before the final words had sealed the lady's last rest, two servants waited with shovels for the digging of another grave. Dr. Gager had died, and Mrs. Phillips. Arbella's maid Molly had outlived her mistress but an hour. Goodman Bennett, Goodwives James and Turner, and Mr. Shepley, and some indentured servants, all had died this week.

And to what purpose, thought Phebe. What had they accomplished here? Where were Arbella's beauty and courage now, and where her baby that might have been born to gentleness and happy childhood in the castle of his ancestors? Buried in the wilderness, beneath a stone for fear of wolves.

She turned and started up the path across the fields. I'm going home, she thought. I'll make Mark see reason, and if he won't—I'll go alone, until he's ready to come back to me. Nothing can make me bring forth my poor child in this enemy land. She stopped and leaned against a tree, seeing against the coarse dry stubble at her feet a shimmering vision. She saw her mother and father holding out their arms to her from the doorway and smiling welcome. She saw the great hall behind them garlanded with roses and ivy as it had been last St. John's Day, and heard the blithe singing of her sisters at their spinning.

She felt the smoothness of the lavender-scented sheets on her own carved oaken bed, and she saw herself and the babe lying there together, safe and tended by her mother's knowing hands, while the mellow sunshine—not fierce and scorching like here—flickered through the mulberry leaves and the diamond-paned windows. She had not cried before, but now a sob burst through her throat, and she stumbled blindly on the path, until a hand touched her shoulder.

She raised her bowed head to see Mr. Johnson beside her. His cheeks, no longer pink, had fallen into sharp grooves. His thin blond hair was uncombed, and from his black habit he had cut away every button and shred of lace.

"Mistress Honeywood," he said, speaking through stiff lips, "will you come back with me, I've something to give you."

She nodded a little, and they walked silently together along the highway past the green to Arbella's house. Phebe cast one look at the plank bedstead on which the Lady had died, and turned away, standing by the door.

Isaac Johnson opened a drawer of the little oak table. "She loved you much," he said, his voice so hoarse that Phebe must lean forward to hear.

"And I her, sir."

He fumbled distractedly amongst several letters which he brought from the drawer. "I go straight back to Boston. There's so much to do —I doubt that I've much time before I join her. The sickness gripes at my bowels. It is the Lord's will. Here are letters she left—one that treats of you. You shall have it."

He held out to her a folded sheet of paper. Phebe took it and opened it, staring at the lines of clear delicate writing.

"I cannot read it—sir," she said very low.

"Aye—to be sure." He snatched it back from her, and she saw that he was impatient to be alone with his sorrow.

"'Twas meant for her sister, Lady Susan Humphrey, but never finished." He steadied his voice and began to read.

"'No word yet from home, so I write thee again, dear sister, perchance to send this by the Master of the *Lion*. I try to keep my thoughts from harking back, but oft-times I cannot, this to my shame, for there be many here who are braver.

"'There is great sickness, and I do pray for the babe I carry. I am much alone and endeavour to strengthen my spirit in the Lord God who led us here. He gives me solace, and in especial hath vouchsafed to me a friend. This, one Phebe Honeywood, wedded to one of the adventurers, and naught but a simple yeoman's daughter, but a most brave and gentle lass. She is not as illumined by Grace as I could wish. . . .'"

Isaac paused, started to say something, but sighed instead, and went on, " 'Yet she is of fine and delicate spirit, and God is closer to her than she knows. She hath, I confess, been inspiration to me—having a most sturdy courage to surmount any disaster and follow her man anywhere, and found a lasting home.

" 'O, my dear sister, it is such as she who will endure in my stead, to fulfil our dream of the new free land, such as she whose babes will be brought forth here to found a new nation—while I . . . too feeble and faint-hearted . . .'"

Isaac's voice cracked. "That's all." He held the letter out again. "Keep it in remembrance of her."

Phebe could not raise her eyes; red had flooded up her cheeks beneath the slow tears. "Our dear Lady misjudged me," she whispered; "I have no courage—indeed, she did not know . . ."

Isaac was stirred from his own grief by her face. "God will strengthen you, mistress," he said gently. "Trust in Him."

He rose, putting out his hand. She took it blindly and, curtsying, turned and left him alone. She went back to the wigwam and, throwing herself down on the pallet, lay staring up at the ragged rush thatching.

Arbella's letter rested beneath her bodice on her heart, and seemed to whisper its words—"It is such as she who will endure—to fulfil our dream. . . ."

She thought of the promise Arbella had asked of her in the first days of her sickness. "Promise me you'll not give up, no matter what may happen." She had not promised.

It's not fair, cried Phebe to the gentle yearning voice, and lying there alone on the pallet, she vanquished the voice with a dozen hot refutations. This founding a new land, this search for a purer religion was not *her* dream. To her God had made no special revelation. And as for Mark—would it not be wiser to free him for a while from her hampering presence—hers and the babe's, until he either tired of the venture, or had made a really suitable place for them? It was no disgrace to go home, every homebound ship was crammed with those who had seen the pointless folly of the venture. The Lady Arbella, herself too weak for survival, had no right to appoint Phebe her surrogate.

The August afternoon flattened under a blistering sun. Beneath the wigwam's thatching the heat gathered stifling and fetid with the smell of the swamps. Once slow footsteps plodded down the path outside toward the Burial Point. Phebe heard the sound of sobbing and one low cry of anguish that faded into nothing. Then again there was no sound but the rasp of locusts and the rustle of the close-pressing forest.

I shall find the Master of the *Lion*, she thought, starting up at last. The *Lion* would sail as soon as there were fair winds.

Phebe washed her face and hands and smoothed her hair. She took the letter from her bodice and flung it in her bridal chest, slamming the lid. She threw open the batten door, and on the earthen threshold stopped dead.

"Oh, dear God," she whispered. "I cannot." And she sank slowly to her knees between the oak door frames. She knelt there, facing the eastern horizon, while behind Salem the sun sank slowly into the untracked forests of the New World.

God did not seem to speak to her. She felt no explanation or comfort even. But there was certainty.

When Mark returned from his expedition to Marblehead he found Phebe changed, very silent and with a grim set to her mouth. She listened acquiescently but without comment to his enthusiasm for his new plan, and his satisfaction that through Mr. Allerton's influence he had easily obtained a grant of five acres in Marblehead from the Salem authorities, who had little interest in that remote section of their plantation.

She remarked only that it did seem wise to move from Salem town, and the sooner they could move the better. She submitted to the remaining weeks in Salem and to Mark's frequent preparatory absences in Marblehead with an unquestioning fortitude. Since the day when she had received Arbella's letter and finally put all thoughts of going home behind her, she had passed beyond personal fear. Yet the stench of fear hung over the whole colony. Daily disasters battered all the settlements, and no day passed without a death.

In Charlestown it was no better. Governor Winthrop sent word that they were starving, rotted with disease and lacking medicine. He proclaimed a Fast Day throughout the Colony with a view to softening the Divine Chastisement. But Providence still scourged them.

Four weeks after Arbella's death a home-bound ship touched at Salem and brought news from Boston that Isaac Johnson, too, had died and had been buried in the lot by his unfinished house.

When Phebe heard this news she went to her bride chest and, drawing out Arbella's letter, gazed at it long and earnestly. What else besides this piece of paper was there left now of the Lady Arbella? Phebe raised the letter to her cheek, then wrapped it in her wedding handkerchief and put it back at the bottom of the bride chest. Nor did she ever mention the letter to Mark.

The Honeywoods were fortunate in escaping illness; but as September went by they did not also escape malice and envy from their fellow townsmen. During their last days in Salem there were murmurs against them, and slanting dark looks. They had not tried to join the congregation; they were virtually, by their own admission, no better than Papists. And why, in this case, should the Lord allow them immunity from the general sickness? Unless indeed it was not the Lord, but some Satanic power in league with them.

Phebe, openly goaded one day at the town spring by an old crone called Goody Ellis, answered that perhaps the milk from her cow and the abundance of fish caught by Mark filled their bellies and made them better able to withstand sickness. Goody Ellis brushed this aside as nonsense, and made vicious allusions to witchcraft. Phebe was glad enough to be leaving.

There were no women at Marblehead yet. Mark told her, except the squaws in the Indian village over Derby Fort side. And he worried about this for the time when her pains should come upon her. "But I'll get you a midwife from Salem, if I must give her all my silver," he promised, and she agreed indifferently.

On October 8th, the Honeywoods left the wigwam and, descending the path to the landing-place, set out at last for their new home.

Mark had hired a shallop and boatman from the fishing settlement on Salem Neck, and this also conveyed all their goods, except Betsy. The cow must wait in Salem until Mark could lead her around by land —six miles of rough Indian trail through the forests.

It was a fair sparkling day of a kind new to them—for autumn in England held no such vibrance—a freshness of blue and gold on the water, freshness of red and gold on the trees. This buoyancy in the air seemed to bathe one in a tingling expectation, it smelled of salt and sunshine and hope, and Phebe knew a faint return of youthful zest for the first time since Arbella had died.

Scudding before the wind, they swished by Derby Fort Point, and Phebe was pleased to see that from this offshore angle it no longer resembled the headland at home. At Marblehead all would be new and there would be no memories.

They rounded another heavily wooded point, where Mark said there lived a fisherman called John Peach. They veered south-west between two small islands and lost the wind. The boatman and Mark took to their oars, and presently, the tide being high, their prow grated far up the shingle of a little harbour.

Phebe jumped out, careless that she wet her feet or the hem of her blue serge skirts. While the men unloaded the boat she stood on the beach, staring. The sunlight fell warm on her back, duplicating a warmth in her heart. For in that first moment she felt a liking for the place. It was snug here in this little harbour with its two guardian points and tiny sheltering islands, and just beyond them there was grandeur—the whole blue sweep of the Atlantic stretching to the white horizon. Her senses seemed sharpened to a new delight. The sucking of the wavelets on the shingle, the water-born cry of a sea-gull gave her pleasure, and in her nostrils there was the smell of pine trees and salt, mingled with the faint pungency of drying fish. She looked for its source, and saw on the northern curve of the little cove two spindly wooden frames and a shabby, hulking figure crouching over them.

"The fish-flakes," said Mark, seeing her puzzled gaze. He laughed. "That'll be Thomas Gray turning the splits. He's a bit of a knave and generally in liquor, but I've cause to be grateful to him."

Phebe nodded. Mark had told her of the help given by Thomas Gray and John Peach in the building of a shelter. Phebe resigned herself to making do with another wigwam, but seeing Mark's air of mystery and excitement now her hopes rose.

He led her a hundred yards back from the beach through a tangle of ruby sumach and wild asters to a modest clearing. Then he paused and waited, and Phebe did not fail him.

"Why, Mark, love—but it's a real mansion you've builded!" she cried, clapping her hands together. Indeed, it was hardly that. A two-room cabin, topped with thatching, but the walls were solid; framed in sturdy New England pine, faced by pine weather-boarding, and all hewn by Thomas Gray, who had knowledge of carpentry.

Together the three men had built the central chimney of the field stone so abundant here, and cemented the chinks with clay. The six small windows were still unfinished, the thatching of rushes pulled from a near-by pond was ragged and thin, but the thatch poles were of good barked hickory, and the rafters all ready for a permanent roofing later. Inside Phebe was delighted to find a real floor of wide pine planking, and the walls snugly sheathed with soft pine boards.

"It's marvellous!" she cried, running between the two rooms. "I never thought to find you so skilled." And she kised Mark gratefully, indifferent to the grinning boatman who was busy hauling their goods from the shallop.

Mark accepted her delight and gloried in it. He well knew that her family had thought him feckless, and unlikely to provide good care for their daughter. The quick building of this solid house was something of a triumph. To be sure, he had had help: from Allerton's men on the *White Angel*, particularly the ship's carpenter, and then from the two fishermen here.

Exultantly he showed her around their kingdom. Their land adjoined that of Allerton's, where he proposed soon to establish his fishing-stage, and also that of the Bay Company's English governor, Mathew Craddock, who had never left or proposed to leave the Old Country, but bought many likely parcels of land in the new.

Mark pointed out to her their well, so convenient to the house door. How fortunate they had been to find sweet water so soon, and so near the salt. Here would be the privy—here the shed for Betsy. See how many trees they had, three great chestnuts, four elms and a pine, rare luck for this rocky promontory.

Here behind the house on the slope to the Little Harbour was rich soil for a vegetable plot. And here to the south, a stone's throw from the house, was the sea again, the restless deep waters of the Great Harbour. Phebe longed to return to the house and start the placing of their furniture, but Mark held her beside him on the rock-strewn beach.

"This harbour is big enough for a fleet and deep too. Better than six fathom at ebb tide. And mind you—look how sheltered it is! See the spit of land across?" She nodded obediently. " 'Tis a great neck with pasture and marble cliffs on t'other side to quell the sea—and down there to the south, a most fair haven, and Master Allerton says the day'll not linger when we see it teem with shipping."

"For sure it will," said Phebe, and tried to speak with interest. While

56

they stood there the sun had set behind them and the air grown chill. The harbour filled with shadows, and the careless sighing of the waves seemed to increase the solitude. Mark, deep in musing, did not move. Then from the far-off forest side towards Salem she heard the long-drawn howl of a wolf. She shivered and put her hand on Mark's arm. "We have much to do inside."

He turned and helped her up the little bank. She was growing somewhat clumsy and uncertain in her steps.

That winter was one of plodding hardships, and now and again a sharp peak of danger. But Phebe found solace in her home. She kept her two rooms swept and garnished with housewifely pride. When all their goods were at last unpacked, and supplemented by Mark's carpentry of plank table, bedstead and stools, it was not ill-furnished. She had a shelf for her shining pewter, the mugs, platter and salt-cellar. The wooden trenchers were ranged beneath with her pewter spoons and candlesticks. To be sure, she had no candles as yet, or means of making them. The fire gave light enough, or in emergencies pine-knot flares as the Indians used them.

Her kitchen hearth was her special pride, wide and deep enough to have roasted an ox, furnished with the much-travelled andirons, and a stout green lug-pole from which hung her two iron pots. There was colour, too, in this common room from the ears of red and orange Indian corn hung up to dry, and a sparkle of cleanliness from the white beach sand on the floor.

The other room besides the bed held chests and provisions until a lean-to could be built for the latter, but it, too, had its cheerful fire and plenty of iridescent-flamed driftwood to burn in it.

The two fishermen, Thomas Gray and John Peach, found cheer in the Honeywood home, and were grateful for such hospitality as Phebe could provide. They were unlike each other in every way, and before the visit of Isaac Allerton with his great plans, and the subsequent arrival of the Honeywoods, had had little to do with each other. Each had built himself a cabin on the shore half a mile from the other, each had in England learned something of rude carpentry and fishing. There was no other resemblance. John Peach was a meagre wisp of a young man from the West Country, who spoke rarely and wore a look of settled melancholy. Some early tragedy had soured him and made him emigrate. He never spoke of the past, and the Honeywoods learned nothing of his early life.

Thomas Gray was as garrulous and rowdy as his fellow settler was restrained. No inner love of solitude had driven him to this secluded point, but the intense disapproval of the Salemites, who wanted none of him. He had come over with Roger Conant in twenty-three, and sober or half-drunk he was an excellent fisherman. Wholly drunk, he embodied all the failings most abhorred by the ministers.

He brawled, he wenched, he blasphemed, he was given to fits of lewd and unseemly mirth directed at godly members of the congregation.

During the seven years since his landing he had roistered his way through most of the new settlements—from Cape Ann to Beverley, to

Nantasket and Salem. In none had he found welcome. Marblehead had been his solution. Though under Salem jurisdiction, the authorities were so far too busy with their home problems to concern themselves with the outlying districts. Gray found good fishing and convenience to Salem, where he might sell or barter his fish and obtain enough supplies of "strong water" to make his solitary nights more cheerful.

He was a large, and, except when liquor released a violent temper, a good-natured man. Phebe deplored his coarse speech and coarser jests, but both she and Mark liked him.

The Honeywoods kept Christmas Day, a celebration which would have outraged the rest of the colony had anyone known it.

On December 20th, Mark had most providentially shot a wild turkey, which had wandered down to the shore in search of shrimps. Phebe invited the two fishermen to dine and plunged into preparations.

At first the contrast between these preparations and those last year had saddened her so that she almost lost heart, and she weakened into thoughts of home for the first time since August. Christmas had always meant weeks of excited anticipation in the kitchen—where she and her mother supervised the making of the mince-meat, the cakes, and pastries, the boar's head, the snap-dragons, and the wassail bowl—and outside—the ceremony of cutting the Yule log, the gathering of holly and mistletoe, the midnight procession to the sweet-smelling, candle-lit church. Then there were the visits of the mummers in ludicrous costumes, the waits gathered outside the windows and singing the old carols, while inside and out there were dances and the kisses and laughter.

Here, a two-room cabin in the wilderness, and no sound but the waves and a rising winter wind.

"It's folly to try," she said to herself while she stood in the bitter cold and pulled pine boughs from one of their trees. Tears sprang to her eyes and chilled on her cheeks. She wrapped her cloak tight around her swollen figure and walked despondently back to the house. It was Mark who cheered her. Her made her sit and drink a cup of sack that warmed her. He applauded the pine branches, and stuck them on the pegs that held his musket, telling her they were as pretty as holly.

He seemed always light-hearted these days, and was full of plans. With Tom Gray's sporadic help he was building himself a rude shallop; it should be finished by spring, if the winter were not too severe. He looked forward to Allerton's coming. He had been fortunate in finding food. Oysters now, and he pointed to a piggin full of gnarled bluish shells. He had found a bed, which was exposed at ebb tide. "They'll do well to stuff the turkey with, sweetheart," he said, and she smiled again, heartened by his eagerness.

So she stuffed the turkey with oysters and corn meal, and roasted it on a green sapling spit hung on the andiron hooks. The boiled pudding was also of cornmeal, sweetened with all her remaining store of currants, and enriched by Betsy's milk. And in one of her iron pots they concocted a makeshift wassail bowl of beer and brandy and a pinch of her jealously guarded spices.

The guests arrived at noon. Thomas Gray, already something un-steady on his feet, lurched over the rocks through a fine sprinkling of snow, and singing at the top of his voice—"Here we come a-wassailing, among the leaves so green!" He had stuck a gull feather in his Mon-mouth cap, tied a bunch of cedar to his filthy leather doublet, and he held in his hand a fishing-pole from which dangled a huge slab of dried cod.

"Merry Christmas to 'ee—Mistress," he roared at Phebe. "I've brought un a gooding, my best dun-fish. 'Twill be fine for thy belly and what's within it."

Phebe coloured and thanked him. John Peach came in quietly; but even his melancholy eyes lightened at the sight and smell of the great turkey, golden brown on the spit.

"We maun sing—sing—sing," shouted Thomas, helping himself from the wassail bowl and banging his mug on the table. "Raise thy voices, split uns gullets, 'till they hear us in Salem. The snivelling puk-ing whoresons."

Mark laughed and, clinking his mug against Gray's, complied in his melodious baritone.

"Wassail, wassail, all over the town,
    Our bread it is white and our ale it is brown . . ."

Phebe joined in, and even Peach after a while in a whispering mono-tone. They sang all the verses in the old way, lifting their mugs and bowing to each object mentioned. For "A good crop of corn," they bowed to the drying ears by the hearth. "Here's health to the ox," and they bowed towards the shed where Betsy munched her Christmas ration of salt hay.

For "Here's to the maid in lily-white smock," they gave Phebe courtly bows. "In truth," shouted Thomas, slapping his thigh, "she's no maid by the look of her, but we'll greet 'ee none the less."

They ate and they drank and they sang. The snow stopped and the wind roared louder. It blew from the north-east and piled the mount-ing breakers into the Great Harbour. The men grew still a moment, all listening. "Are the boats pulled up high enough, d'you think?" asked Mark uneasily.

"For sure they be," answered Thomas. "This'll be no storm. Coom sing again—we havena had 'The Bellman,' nor the 'Boar's Head,' yet."

But the other two men looked at each other and stood up. Peach nodded and buttoned his doublet. Mark, full of wassail and none too steady, followed the fisherman out into the cold dusk to see to the boats.

Thomas Gray promptly fell off his stool, and lay on the floor snor-ing. Phebe began to straighten up the room.

The feast had gone well. For an hour or so they had almost captured the richness and gaiety of a real Christmas. She had thought of them at home almost in triumph, saying to them, "See, we are not so bar-barous here, nor to be pitied."

But now she saw how flimsy a shell had held their gaiety. The wind rose and the shell was shattered. At home the rising wind meant another log on the fire, another round of punch and a heightening of snug comfort.

Here it meant danger. She pulled her cloak around her and went out into the raw bitter cold to the shed to milk Betsy. She leaned her forehead against the warm flank, while her aching fingers fumbled on the teats. Thank God, the cow had proved sturdy. She did well enough on the salt hay and bran they had brought from Salem.

Above the hissing of the milk into the wooden bucket and the increasing pound of the waves, both woman and cow heard another sound. Betsy shivered and tossed her head.

"Hush," whispered Phebe, though the flesh of her spine crept as it always did. "The wolves can't get at you here."

The shed was strong, and the wolves had never yet come down on the Point.

To soothe Betsy she began to sing the old children's carol of "The Friendly Beasts." Often she had heard her mother sing it to the baby.

And next Christmas, thought Phebe, will I be singing it to mine? But the baby did not seem real.

"Aye, dear God, I wish it were over," she whispered. Her hands fell from the udder. She picked up the heavy bucket, and staggered with it back to the house. She must leave for Salem soon, if the baby were to be born there.

But each succeeding winter day the journey was impossible. It could only be made by boat. Thomas Gray's shallop had been battered, though fortunately not lost, in the Christmas storm. John Peach had only a skiff too small to fight the winter gales which blew steadily through January.

On the first day of February the wind had dropped at last and a glittering sunshine dazzled on the snow patches. The waters of the two harbours calmed to glancing ripples filmed along the shore by brittle ice, and Phebe knew that they might set forth for Salem.

She knew also that it was too late. An agonizing backache had awakened her at dawn. By noon she was in full labour. Mark, helpless and frightened, paced back and forth from the bed, where he clumsily smoothed her forehead and murmured endearments which she did not hear, to the kitchen where he tended a roaring fire and kept a pot of water boiling.

Boiling water he had heard to be needed in child-bed, but he didn't know why and he knew nothing else of the procedure. He dare not leave Phebe to summon the other men, but John Peach presently came of himself to tell them he had the skiff ready.

"No good now," Mark groaned; "her pains are already monstrous hard. I don't know what to do."

A smothered cry came to them from the bedroom, and the sweat sprang out on his forehead. He ran to Phebe. She was panting, her eyes stared without recognizing him, the pupils dilated to black holes.

An hour went by and he knelt beside the bed. Sometimes she seized his hand as though it were a block of wood without life, and clutched at it so violently that his great bones cracked.

Sometimes she tore at the stout darnacle coverlet, and her nails ripped gashes in the material.

At five the pains seemed to lessen a little and Phebe drowsed. There was a knock on the door. Mark opened it to see Thomas Gray and an Indian squaw.

Gray, sober for once, stepped forward. "Look 'ee, Honeywood, John Peach come to me cot saying thy good wife's pains're on her, and 'ee fair distraught. This squaw's got brat of 'er own, and must know summat of birthing. So I brung 'er."

Mark's intense relief at the sight of a woman, any woman, was nearly eclipsed by astonishment. Only a few Marblehead Indians had remained to brave the winter, and they kept severely to themselves over by Tagmutton Cove. Nor did they allow their women to roam. This young squaw in her doeskin dress, with a mantel of beaver fur on her shoulders, was not uncomely, though her bronze skin was faintly pitted by the smallpox. She gave Mark a deprecatory smile, which showed even white teeth.

"Name's Winny-push-me, or summat like that," said Thomas. "I call her Winny." As Mark still looked astonished he added, "She's my doxy." He gave the squaw a pinch on her backside and she giggled.

"But, Tom—it's rash!" Mark cried. "We daren't offend the Indians, we're so few here . . ."

Thomas went to the fire and rubbed his hands. "Ah, ye needna fret. She's a widder woman, they care naught wot she do. I've bedded with her off and on for better'n a year."

A moan from Phebe recalled Mark. He took the squaw by the arm. "Go see what you can do." The woman understood his gestures, and Mark followed her to the bed.

Phebe cried out and shrank as she saw the dark face and felt the alien hands on her, but through the red surges of renewed pain she heard Mark's voice. "She'll help you, sweetheart. Let her do what she will."

Winnepashemic was a skilled midwife, a role which often fell to the tribe's widows. She watched Phebe's pains carefully, nodded and produced from her bosom a leather pouch. From it she drew a sharp bone knife and a small leather thong. These she laid on the floor, to be used later. She got hot water from the kitchen pot and mingled with it a powdered herb which she forced Phebe to drink. In a few minutes Phebe's pains increased in violence and frequency. Winnepashemic nodded again, satisfied, and pulled up the blankets.

Half an hour later the baby was born. The squaw deftly cut the cord with her bone knife and bound the stump with the thong; then she wrapped the baby in her own beaver mantle and carried it to the kitchen.

She thrust the bundle toward Mark. "Man," she said, beaming. Mark, whose body dripped with sweat and whose hands shook, stared at her blankly, but Thomas jumped up and pulled apart the beaver wrapping.

"So it be!" he shouted. "A fine boy, red as a strawberry an' plump as an oyster." He clapped Mark on the shoulders. "Ye can smile now, my hearty young stud."

Mark looked at the baby, at the smiling faces of the fisherman and the squaw. He mopped his forehead with the back of his sleeve and went in to Phebe, walking on tiptoe. In his great chest was a hard fear. The sound of her screams were still in his ears.

She lay so quiet and flat on the bed that his mouth went dry and he could not speak. Then he saw her drowsy lids lift, and she, too, smiled at him.

"No need to fear, Mark," she said dreamily. Her smile seemed to come from a secret distance. But she saw his need and made greater effort. "It's all over. Aren't you content we've a fine boy?"

"But Phebe—it w-was fearful, I thought—thought . . ."

He fumbled for her hand, clumsy in his pity, and amazed that she could smile that little secret smile.

"Aye"—she squeezed his hand, quieting his restless fingers—"it was bad, bad as I always feared. But I got through it—and the babe. We're strong."

He was humbled by the triumphant pride in her last words. He saw her exalted and far from him. Nor did he know that above the natural triumph of accomplished childbirth, she had private cause to exult. Though her next words might have given him a clue.

"You won't mind, Mark, if we name him Isaac?"

"Isaac?" he repeated. He had thought, in the few times he thought of it at all, that the baby if a boy would be Mark again, or perhaps for her father—Joseph. Isaac? Isaac Allerton. His frown cleared. It would be fine compliment to the man who had settled them there; it would increase his interest in them when he finally arrived himself.

"For Master Johnson," she said softly. "Please." During the hours past, the pain had wiped out all thought of anything but itself. She had not thought of her mother, she had not thought of God. She had been as beast-like as Goody Carson on the ship. But now she knew that did not matter. And since it had finished, she had felt the Lady Arbella near her, smiling a gentle, happy smile.

Mark was not pleased, but he could deny her nothing now. And later, if he cautioned her to silence, Mr. Allerton would believe the boy named for him. Mark bent over and kissed Phebe gently on the mouth.

In the September of 1636 Phebe, dressed in her crimson farrandine, and bridal cap and neckwear of the Mechlin lace, hurried along the Harbour Lane to Redstone Cove, as eager as little Isaac for the day's festivity. The child danced with excitement, and she held him tightly by the hand or he would have darted on ahead and maybe soiled the new suit she had made him from her blue serge gown. Yet, were it not for the cooing baby she carried on her left arm, Phebe felt she might have run and danced like Isaac.

The sun, warm and golden as brandy, poured down from an azure sky, but it was not too hot. A small crisp breeze blew down the harbour, and the Neck had moved so near in the September air, it seemed a reaching hand might touch the massed green trees across the water.

"There she be—there's the ship!" shouted the child. Phebe nodded and smiled, and paused to look a moment before scrambling down amongst the rocks to find a sitting place for the launching.

There she was, finished at last, the pride of all Marblehead. A great fair ship, 120 tons burden, the largest yet built in the Colony as Mark so often boasted. Fully rigged, she poised lightly on the waves like a black swan, and across her stern ran her name in glowing red letters, *Desire*. Ah yes—well-named, thought Phebe, settling herself on a rock and spreading her crimson skirts; for more than a year the village had centred its hopes and dreams upon this ship. And Mark more than any of the others.

She saw him now leaning against the taffrail on the high poop-deck, talking to Jemmie White and John Bennet, and they all held mugs in their hands. He waved to her and shouted, "Hulloa, Phebe, I'll be right down to you. Does the boy know his part?"

She waved back, and made little Isaac wave. As the first child born in Marblehead, he had been appointed to christen the vessel. As the son of a man of consequence, too, thought Phebe proudly. Mark had thrown himself heart and soul into this venture, and contributed every penny he had and labour too, working day after day with the other men on the sturdy oak hull. He dreamed of his share of the profits from her cargoes, and he announced that he had found his real profession at last. He would be shipwright and owner.

He had, during these six years of their settlement here, done fairly well at the fishing; he had his own shallop and his own fish-flakes at the foot of his land on Little Harbour, but Isaac Allerton's larger projects had never been realized. True, Allerton came to Marblehead and established his fishing-stage, but soon the remote little settlement bored him; there was small scope for his ambitions, and then misfortunes beset him—his house burned down, and the *White Angel* was lost with all her cargo. He became morose and restless, and in 1635, having deeded all his Marblehead property to his son-in-law, Moses Maverick, Master Allerton disappeared in the direction of the New Haven Colony, and Massachusetts knew him no more. Then Mark had said "Good riddance"; feeling that he had misjudged Allerton's worth, and having in any case small interest in working for someone else.

How many changes here, in how short a time, thought Phebe. Eleven women now in Marblehead besides herself, and twenty-eight men, and the children. She looked down on the sleeping baby on her lap—small Mark. His birthing had been aided by Dorcas Peach, a jolly stout widow from Saugus, suddenly and surprisingly married by the melancholy young fisherman, John Peach. And the birthing had been easy, very different from that of Isaac.

And there were other houses now in Marblehead—huts and cabins strung along the waterfront all the way from John Peach's Point to Bartol's Head, but no house except Mr. Maverick's so fine as the Honeywoods'.

Aye, I'm content, thought Phebe, watching Mark clamber down the ladder from the ship and come towards her. How handsome he looked as he swaggered along the shingle, taller and stronger than all the other men, and how boyish still for all his thirty years. He had a streak of pitch across his cheek, and some of the points on his doublet hung loose.

"You're heedless as the boy is," she scolded fondly, wiping at his cheek. "Nay—don't tumble him about." For Mark had seized his elder son and thrown him high in the air. "You'd not have him queasy for the launching."

"God blast it—no!" cried Mark with a boisterous laugh. "But he's no get of mine, trollop, if he hasn't a strong stomach." He lowered the delighted child in a great swoop, then stumbled and caught himself.

"Oh, Mark," cried Phebe between reproach and amusement, "not tipsy so soon! Had you nothing better to do up there on the ship than guzzle."

"No. All's ready and waiting for high water, and I'll drink as I please. Come, poppet, no long face. This is the day to rejoice. I'm happy as I never thought to be." He put his arm around her waist and squeezed it hard. "All goes well for us, at last."

"Aye, for sure it does," she said, smiling back at him. For whence but from womanish cowardice had come that little moment of foreboding, a chill that crept along her spine and vanished in the brightness around her. Mark patted his wife's shoulder, poked a finger at the baby; then, drawn as by a lodestone, walked back to the ship and climbed aboard.

The cove was filling now, in the village all work had ceased and they came over the cliff and down the rocky path, each dressed in best attire, the Marblehead women and the children and the few men who were not about the ship. Some were shouting, some singing, and all elated by the completion of their community project.

Young Remember Maverick, Moses's bride, radiant in her green paragon, ran towards Phebe crying, "What, here already Phebe? Look, d'you see up there 'pon the ledge? I vow those are Salem men."

Phebe followed the girl's gaze, to see two peering figures in sad-coloured clothes. They were approaching the cove tentatively.

"They've sailed over to view the launching, no doubt," said Phebe, laughing. "Just so, they keep their distance. They'll get short-shrift if Mark sees them."

"Or any of our men—ah, I thought so." For Tom Gray reeled down the path and stopped short at the sight of the strangers.

"We want no foreigners here," he shouted. "Snivelling whoreson spies. Get ye back to your psalm whining and your magistrating. Ye couldna build a ship like thisun, if ye strained till your arses burst."

And he picked up a large stone. The Salemites retreated hastily behind a tree. "Oh hush, Tom," whispered Phebe, not for disapproval of his sentiments, but because he would certainly be hauled up before the Salem Court again. Salem considered this rocky outpost of its own tight community to be a godless and intractable stepchild, and concerned itself with the renegade only for purposes of discipline. There was as yet no meeting house in Marblehead, nor preacher, and few who felt the need of either.

Tom let fly the rock, which bounced off the tree, and would have thrown another, but Mr. Maverick appeared, and taking in the situation, shrugged his shoulders, saying decisively, "Let them be, Tom, we've better matters to be about."

The tide was nearly high. There were shouts from the men on the ship, and the half-dozen who remained on shore swarmed over the ways and began to knock at the retaining planks. The women clustered together, staring at the ship, their hearts beating with pride and expectancy.

They stared at the oak hull made from their own trees, at the two towering masts cut from the finest stand of spruce in Essex county, the quarter mile of rope in the rigging, all imported from Bristol, the shining paint on her hull, tediously mined from the Indian paint mine back of Beverley, and the sails—their cloth had come from England, too, and for its purchase there had been many a sacrifice made.

How many feet of cloth, thought Phebe, were represented by the sale of poor Betsy's only calf? But every Marbleheader there had had part in the building of the *Desire*; poor as they were—and even the Mavericks were poor by Salem or Boston standards—they had willingly pooled their hard-won shillings.

They had done it all by themselves with the fierce independence which had drawn them here, men and women from Cornwall and the other West counties, and from the Channel Islands—disparate beings, some as rough and uncouth as the savages, some of tenderer stamp, but held together by a dual bond—the love of freedom and the sea.

The harbour water lapped up to the pitch mark they had made upon a rock. The hammering increased in volume. Little Isaac tugged at his mother's skirt. "See Dada," he cried shrilly, pointing his plump finger and hopping up and down. Phebe tilted her head high to see Mark foremost of three young men who were swarming up the rigging on the mainmast. Phebe caught her breath but smiled. How like Mark! He would never submit to standing tamely on the deck while the beloved ship was launched. But the others stopped at the crow's-nest, while Mark went on, until he perched astride the yard of the topgallant-sail, and waved his cap in exultant gesture. Again a chill touched her. But why must he always be reckless, in everything excessive and trying to beat the others? Why could he not . . . ?

"Well, Mistress Honeywood, is the boy ready?" Moses Maverick stood before her, holding out the uncorked flask of claret.

"Oh yes," she said quickly. "Go with him, dear."

Isaac's chubby fist closed on the bottle's neck, and while Maverick held him up on the platform he obediently lisped. "I christen thee *Desire*," and sprinkled wine on the great wooden wall of the stern.

The ship started, she slid gently down the greased ways, and the tide leapt up to meet her, but as she settled into the blue harbour waters she gave one sideways lurch, and from the watching crowd there came a hissing gasp of horror. The ship righted herself at once, but Mark, who had leaned out far to see his son perform the triumphant ceremony, lost his balance on the yard and came hurtling down to the deck below.

Mark was unconscious for many days, and after he came to himself his mind was clouded and he could move neither of his legs. Moses Maverick sent a shallop to Salem and brought back a physician, but that worthy gentleman, after examining Mark, shook his head and said he believed the backbone was crushed. He could do nothing.

Phebe received this verdict in silence. Her brown eyes took on a chill and stony look; she neither prayed nor lamented, and the physician thought her unfeeling. So did others who, stopping at the door to give sympathy and food, were received with tight-lipped thanks.

Dorcas Peach, who helped her with the nursing, and Tom Gray, who neglected his own livelihood to save Phebe from the rougher tasks—these knew better.

They saw the unfailing tenderness which she showed to Mark, who was often fretful and sometimes swept by violent rages in which he cursed Phebe or little Isaac, making of them objects to be battered for his helpless rage at fate. While his mind was clouded from the fearful pain he babbled incessantly about the ship, thinking himself on board, and it was Phebe, who, indifferent to the ridicule of some of the towns-people, asked Tom to fashion a giant-sized cradle. And after he had done so and they had lifted Mark's shrunken body into it, Phebe rocked it very slowly, and the gentle motion, mingling in his thoughts with the motion of a ship, did bring relief from the pain.

After a while as he grew stronger the pain receded, and he no longer needed the cradle; then he would lie propped up in bed silent for a day at a time, and once when Phebe came to feed him the evening meal, his brilliant hazel eyes sought hers with a violent determination. And he commanded her to bring him his gun. "Bring it to me, Phebe! I can't live like this." And he struck down at his wizening, nerveless legs. "Half a man. No man." His face contorted and he clutched at her arm. "Phebe, bring me the gun, and when you're widowed there'll be plenty of men to take you and the children. . . ."

Then she slipped her arms around his neck, and held his heavy head against her breast, whispering to him as she did to the little ones, sooth-ing him with a hundred gentle words. "Nay, darling, hush. We'll manage, I know we will. You'll get better. Why, I'll warrant by spring you'll be back in your shallop fishing the bay."

But she knew he would not. Nor for some months, while they lived off the neighbours' offerings, did she know how the black future was to be endured.

The *Desire's* first voyage had been successful. Spain and Portugal welcomed the cargo of salt fish, cured by the New England sun, and tastier than the native Bacalao. The *Desire* returned with oil, wine and salt—and a moderate profit. Mark's share was small, and in it he had now no interest. Phebe dared not mention the ship, for all reminders of his accident provoked attacks of pain and violence far worse than the dull apathy into which he had gradually lapsed.

Phebe spent many days in hesitation and nervous anxiety, all the more acute since she must hide it from Mark, and many nights—she slept now in the loft with the children—she lay till dawn staring up at the black outlines of the rafters. Then she awoke one bleak February morning with her decision made.

She hurried through her tasks, fearful of losing that moment of certainty. She nursed the baby and bundled him in his cradle, she replenished the kitchen fire, and heated the porridge for their breakfast, she tended Mark who lay heavy as a log of yew. He would neither open his eyes nor speak, but he ate a little when she coaxed him, and when she said she must go out for a while, he seized her hand and held it tight —as though in fear to have her leave him.

When Dorcas Peach came over to help, as she did each day, being warm-hearted and having no children of her own as yet, Phebe was waiting already cloaked. She left her household in Dorcas's care and set out northward along the icy-rutted lane until she came to Moses Maverick's.

Mr. Maverick was at home, sitting at a writing table near to the kitchen fire, for the day was bitter cold. He received Phebe kindly, but she saw the corners of his mouth sink in and in his eyes a wariness This did not surprise her. She well knew that her problem was a burdensome one to the settlement.

"And how is your good man today, Mistress Honeywood?" he asked, pulling up a chair for her and seating himself again at the table which was covered with sheets of foolscap.

Phebe's hand twisted itself into a fold of her homespun skirt, but she spoke quietly, seeming to consider the matter. "Why, he's neither better nor worse. His mind is no longer much clouded, but he cannot move his legs. Nor do I think he ever will."

Maverick shook his head. "That's bad. Bad. And he so tall and strong he used to do the work of two. Had he only not been so rash . . ."

He had spoken his thoughts without regard to the listener, for he was one of those to whom Phebe's composure had always seemed unwomanly. He was therefore shocked to see a spasm cross her face, as a stone convulses the still waters of a pool, and in that instant grief looked nakedly from her brown eyes.

"Pardon, mistress!" he cried. "I didn't mean to cause you pain. It does no good to think of the past."

"No," she said, controlled again. "It's because of the future that I came to you."

He drew back into his chair. The wariness returned to his gaze, and he sighed. His young wife, Remember, was fond of Mistress Honeywood, and had much troubled him with questions and speculations as to what would become of the stricken family. Food was not so plentiful that anyone should be asked to provide for four extra mouths. Mark Honeywood's affliction was indeed a cruel drag on the struggling little settlement, which could ill afford to have one of its strongest assets reverse the ledger and become a debit. Far better had he died, thought Maverick; women were scarce, and she might then find a man to take her, for all she was so small and thin and reserved in her ways.

"I think there is but one solution, mistress." He spoke with exasperation and decision. "Return to England! You have people there to care for you?"

Phebe lowered her head and stared at the fire. She was silent so long that he began to feel discomfited. Then she spoke very slowly, so that he leaned forward to catch the words.

"I've thought of it many times. Many times," she repeated slowly.

Then she raised her head and looked at him. "But I cannot go back. Nay," she added with a faint smile, seeing that he thought there was some discreditable reason, "my family would welcome us. They'd care for Mark and provide for me and the children."

"Then why . . . ?" he began, frowning. "You've no Puritan scruples."

She shook her head. "But I can't go. Two things prevent." He waited, still frowning and tapping on the table. After a moment she went on with difficulty.

"I can't go because Mark, the real Mark, wouldn't wish it. He's lost courage now, but I can't take advantage of his weakness. This place was his choice. Our children were born here. We've endured much—and Marblehead has become—home." She paused a moment, then went on swiftly. "The other reason is a promise."

A promise I never made, she thought, seeing the dark stuffy little room in Salem and on the bed the dying lady. And she thought of the letter that lay wrapped in the lawn handkerchief at the bottom of her bride chest.

Maverick crossed his legs and cleared his throat, seeing that she had finished speaking. "Admirable reasons, no doubt, and do you honour —but Mistress Phebe—the practical . . ."

She nodded and cut in. "I know. I've a plan. I want you to apply to the Salem Court for me, for licence to run an ordinary."

"An ordinary?" he repeated slowly, relieved by something practical at last. "You mean to run one in your house? But have you room? Could you do it alone? There are many considerations. Our plantation is yet small to support one."

"I think not." Phebe smiled. "The fishermen and the sailors will certainly welcome one. Tom Gray'll help me. We can build a room for Mark off the kitchen, our other room to be the taproom. Mark will, some day, take an interest, I hope. He can keep the books, and there'll be people around to divert him."

"And how will you buy your stock?"

"From Mark's share in the *Desire*."

Moses stared at her. He had misjudged her. She was neither deficient in feeling nor character. Colour had come into her thin cheeks as she talked, and he saw that she was not deficient in comeliness either.

"You have courage, my dear," he said.

Phebe looked puzzled. "But indeed I haven't," she said earnestly; "not in myself."

Maverick smiled, looking at her with gentleness, understanding why his wife was so fond of her. "Perhaps we never know ourselves, our virtues or our faults. . . ." He uncrossed his legs and stood up. "I believe that you'll somehow manage to keep your home together here, and your plan is practical. I'll give you what help I can."

That May of 1637 Phebe opened her ordinary. Mark had been carried to a chair beside the beer keg in the taproom, and though his face had fallen into deep grooves and bitterness pulled his mouth, he managed to speak to the first customers, Moses Maverick and John Peach. Phebe, in white apron and cap, stood behind the counter, near to Mark, where sometimes, when the strain was too much for him, she touched his shoulder and whispered encouragement.

The taproom, with its rush-strewn floor, its shelves of wooden mugs, its casks of brandy and sack, its tables and benches, showed little resemblance to the bedroom where the Honeywoods had spent their first years. Their bedroom now, duly built by Thomas Gray, lay off the north side of the kitchen, and its windows gave on to the Little Harbour. From it Mark could look across Phebe's garden and watch the landing of slippery cargo at the fishing-stage. He could also watch his elder son, who escaped whenever possible from the chores set him by Phebe to splash in and out of the shallops.

Above the front door of the house Thomas Gray had nailed a small dried hazel bush, as was required by the law to show a licensed ordinary. But Phebe had wished a sign as well and, though her advisers had thought it extravagance, had commissioned a roving painter. The figures beneath the straggling letters were inconclusive—two rigid objects topped by spheres, and between them a bird. The legend was clarifying. It said, the "Hearth and Eagle," and though the Marble-headers ignored the sign and referred to the tavern as "Honeywoods'," it gave Phebe a secret content. Even though she must now receive strangers into her home, yet the andirons were still guardians in the kitchen and on the sign. As for the eagle—that was for the gilt figure-head of the ship *Arbella.*

CHAPTER THREE

A DESCENDANT of the first "Hearth and Eagle" sign creaked and rattled on its iron bracket outside Hesper Honeywood's window, awakening her at sunrise on the morning of April 23rd, 1858.

"Drat that sign!" she said out loud, and muffled her ears with her pillow to shut out the piercing squeal-bang, squeal-bang. Needed oiling again, or better yet take the stupid thing down, as Ma kept saying. Inns didn't have signs like that nowadays, and Johnnie Peach had once made fun of the blurred drawings on it, called it a spitted chicken.

Only Pa wouldn't take it down. He would never change anything.

Hesper yawned and gave up trying to sleep. Ma'd be hollering for her to get up pretty soon, anyway. Awful lot of chores to be done before school. The inn was crammed full and there'd be big doings tonight, what with most of the ship's crew sailing for the spring fare to the Banks tomorrow if this fair wind held. The sign banging away like that meant a good stiff offshore breeze.

Johnnie'd be tickled pink, couldn't wait to sail again now he'd be full sharesman in the *Diana*.

Hesper sighed. Silly to think about Johnnie when he didn't pay her any mind now she was a great girl of sixteen, nor for a long time before that either. Not since she'd gone to dame school, and he'd given up schooling and sailed off on his first fare to the Grand Banks, as a "cuttail." That was five years ago, when he was fourteen, and he'd suddenly gotten ashamed of playing with a girl, even when the rest of the boys in the Barnegat gang didn't know about it.

I wish I was a boy, thought Hesper passionately. Johnnie'd taught her to sail, and she could handle a dory almost as well as any boy, and once when she was ten Johnnie'd lent her some of his clothes and smuggled her on the *Balance* when the ship went down to Boston for the salt. They'd been gone two days, and there was a terrible hullabaloo when they got back. Ma'd tanned her backside so she couldn't sit for a week, but it was worth it.

She heard her mother's heavy tread on the old boards outside in the hall, and there was a sharp rap. "Hurry up, Hes. It's gone six."

Hesper said, "Yes, Ma," and reluctantly slid out of bed on to the braided-rag rug. It had been made by poor old Gran just before she died, out of scraps of sprigged calico and homespun and torn stockings Gran had hoarded like a magpie. It kept the floor's chill off the feet, and it was pretty enough and spotlessly clean because Ma made her wash it once a month; but Hesper despised it. Charity Trevercombe had a red turkey rug so thick you could sink your fingers in it at *her* bedside. But then the Trevercombes were still rich. They'd made a fortune in the China trade and kept some of it too, which was more than the Honeywoods had done. The Honeywoods had only been rich for a while in the middle of the last century, when Moses Honeywood, the shipowner, had built the great new wing to the house, and married off his daughters into some of the foremost families—the Hoopers and the Ornes and the Gerrys. Then the Revolution came and he lost every penny. Charity was pretty, too, the prettiest girl in Marblehead.

Hesper slipped off her long flannel nightgown and shivered. She poured water from a dented pewter pitcher into a chinaware basin, moistened her arms and face and neck, deciding with relief that there wasn't time to wash all over. I wish I wasn't so big, she thought, her discontent growing. She had only recently become conscious of her body, and the consciousness brought nothing but disappointment. She was taller than any other girl at the Academy, five and a half feet— near as tall as Johnnie. And suddenly, in the last year, a lot of—well, bosom. She dried herself and flung on her underclothes. She brushed her hair with violence. Red. Brick-carrot red, curly and springy as wood shavings, and so much of it, below the waist and thick enough when braided to make a hawser, and she had been teased about it since she was a baby. She skinned it all back from her face and slicked the wiry little tendrils down with water, staring into the small mirror, exasperated by a new reminder. It was bad enough to have the Lord afflict her with tallness and that hair, and a squarish face with high cheekbones, and a wide mouth, and light brown eyes that looked almost green in some lights. But why must He refine still further upon an effect already so far removed from prettiness, by endowing her with thick dark eyebrows? She flung the brush and comb on to her bureau, buttoned herself into her brown serge school dress. Well, anyway, the Lord spared me freckles, she thought forlornly. Ma and some of the Dollibers who had sandy hair had the freckles, too. Hesper's skin was a thick dense cream, like, as a schoolmate had once remarked, "the insides of a clam shell." Hesper had tried to believe it a compliment.

She threw her bed together, not bothering to untuck the sheets and hoping Ma would be too busy to look. She slapped on the counterpane and paused at the sound of hoofs and the rumble of heavy wheels outside. She peered through the tiny-paned window at the street, and saw that it was the delivery dray from Medford. Two men were unloading casks of molasses and rum, and carrying them into the taproom. Early, thought Hesper, faintly surprised. They must have driven the team all night. And she hurried downstairs to the kitchen.

Susan called from the taproom where she was supervising the delivery of the casks, "Turn the sausages, start the fish-cakes, and the milk's ready for skimming in the buttery, and hurry for once. The two drummers've to be off for Lynn."

Hesper nodded and flew to the little pot-bellied cook-stove. The fire in the great fireplace would be lit later, but the brick oven was still warm from yesterday and contained pans of swollen bread dough, ready now for baking. She took them out, and put them on the table, stirred the grounds in the huge spouted can of coffee, turned the sausages and fish-cakes again, then ran into the taproom to set the table for the drummers' breakfast. And she was amazed to find her mother standing, stock-still in the centre of the floor, staring at a piece of paper.

"What is it, Ma?" Hesper tried to crane over her mother's shoulder, and saw what appeared to be a regular bill for the rum and molasses, with some lines of brownish writing across the very bottom of it.

"Mind your own business," said Susan, folding up the paper. But she spoke with a hesitancy, most unlike her. "You're too young . . ." She scowled at the paper. "Today of all days with the house full, and a crowd tonight . . . but it must be done . . . someway."

"What must, Ma?" cried Hesper, beside herself with curiosity.

Susan put the piece of paper in her apron pocket. "You'd be a blabber-mouth . . ."

"No, no, Ma . . ."

Susan shook her head, pursed in her lips. "Get on with the work, you'll be late to school." She walked from the taproom, through the kitchen to Roger's study door, and threw it open without knocking.

Hesper, seething with curiosity and the resentment which her mother often aroused in her followed close. The door to her father's study was ajar a crack, she put her ear as close as she dared and listened.

". . . and it's the U.G.," said her mother's voice finishing a sentence. "Written in milk on the bill like the last time. I held it to the fire. There's two of 'em, I guess, and they're coming tonight."

"I'll have nothing to do with it!" cried her father's voice sharply. "I absolutely forbid it."

"Forbid—indeed!" the voice harshened with anger. "You did it last time and you'll do it again."

"That was different, years ago, before they passed the Act. I'll not break the law. I told them I wouldn't."

Hesper heard her mother's heavy hand strike the desk. "Blast and domnation! Since when do Marbleheaders cringe at a law if it's a bad one. They must be desperate or they wouldn't be trying us. It maddens me to have you turn niminy-piminy, chicken-hearted . . ."

"That's enough, Susan. I disliked the last episode, and, after all, my own ancestors were slave owners. Moses Honeywood owned several blacks," said Roger in his nervous, irritable voice. "I'll not have my house used as a station again."

Hesper gasped, pressing closer to the door. So that was it! The U.G. was the "underground railroad."

"You hold with slavery then?" shouted her mother.

"Why no, but I doubt abolitionism's the answer. Let the South take care of its problems, and remember, too, there are many Southern sympathizers here in Marblehead."

"Bah! Some of the shoemen, and maybe the Cubbys, because poor Leah has no mind of her own since her man was drowned, and Nat, that young whelp of hers'd swarm to any view that'd roil decent folks."

"There's no use arguing; I've no more to say."

Hesper heard the familiar sound of pen scatching on paper, and drew back from the door, but not fast enough. Susan burst through, her cheeks red and her little eyes snapping. She stared at her daughter's guilty face and banged the door behind her. "So you've been eavesdropping, Miss. You heard it all?"

Hesper opened her mouth and shut it again, but oddly enough Ma wasn't mad. She sank down in the old Windsor chair, and said very low, "Well, Hes. We'll have to do it alone. The poor things'll be coming, and we can't send 'em back, despite your Pa."

Hesper instantly stifled a pang of loyalty. For surely Pa was wrong in this. It was because he wouldn't read *Uncle Tom's Cabin*, though nearly everyone else in Marblehead had. He wouldn't even read any of Mr. Longfellow's stirring poems like "The Slave in the Dismal Swamp." He only read books by dead people who had lived across the ocean long ago. So he didn't know how terribly the poor slaves suffered, and, anyway, this was so exciting.

"How can we do it, Ma?" she whispered eagerly. "The house'll be full all evening with the 'Bankers' who sail tomorrow. . . ."

"Hush," said Susan sharply, glancing at the banjo clock. "There's those drummers a-coming downstairs. Feed 'em their vittles, and then I'll tell you what to do. You can skip school today."

Hesper waited on the two men, banging plates and spilling coffee in her haste, and for once unrebuked by her mother, who moved automatically through her kitchen work, her sandy brows pulled together in a scowl of concentration.

Her decision once taken, she had not the slightest scruple in deceiving Roger. She had many times before this had to take command, ignoring his uncertainties and evasions, allowing, though with scant tolerance, for his increasing retreat from life. For fifteen years he had been engaged on a rhymed metrical account of the town entitled "Marblehead Memorabilia." But as his treatment of the work entailed so many classical allusions and consequent detours into reference books and source material, he had progressed no farther than the French and Indian wars.

That this poem was to be an apology and justification for a life of outward failure, both his wife and child dimly understood; but to Susan the fecklessness of the project was added exasperation. All his life it had been the same story. As a matter of course, he had been sent to sea on a "Banker" as cook when he was twelve. During the whole of that six weeks' fare he had lain in his bunk in the fo'c'sle seasick and entirely useless.

"I doubt he'll never make a seaman," the skipper had said contemptuously on returning him to his father. Nor did he. He was a clumsy, unwilling fisherman, he had no knack for boats.

Thomas Honeywood, his father, finally accepted these strange shortcomings, though there had never been a Honeywood since the days of Mark and Phebe who had not spent a great part of his life at sea. Thomas decided on a new course. The boy was brilliant at the Academy, and was for ever piddling about with ink and quill, when he was not hidden in the attic with a book. Let him be a scholar then. No matter the money, young Roger should go to Harvard. But nothing came of that either. At Cambridge he made no friends. The other students thought him a queer fish and mimicked his Marblehead dialect, which in fact he hadn't known he had. He responded with anger, and secretly practised many hours to rid himself of it. He studied little, cut many classes, spent all the time he dared in the library, and then he fell ill, he had dull headaches and sudden spasms of unexplained terror in which he sweated and vomited. At the end of his fourth term, he failed all his examinations.

Home he came to Marblehead, and the illness ceased. His father, though bitterly disappointed, said little, but tried to make him useful in the business end of inn-keeping. Here, too, Roger was vague and inattentive, having no interest in figures. Then when he was twenty, attracted both of them by the law of opposites, he married Susan Dolliber, and all Marblehead agreed that it was the only piece of gumption he ever showed.

"Ma—they've gone," whispered Hesper, coming into the kitchen with a tray piled high with dirty dishes. "Have you planned?"

Susan cast a sharp look over the tray, picked up the two quarters which were payment for the breakfasts, and put them in a hinged lacquer box which she kept in a drawer of the old dresser.

"Come in here," she said very low. She pulled her daughter to the left of the great fireplace and through the door of the "Borning Room" —the kitchen bedroom, unused since Gran died, because it was sacred to birth and death and grave illness. She shut the wide-planked oak door. "You'd best read the message," she said, taking the Medford bill from her pocket, " 'fore I burn it."

Hesper peered eagerly at the faint brown letters at the extreme bottom of the page. They said: "2 packages tonight by nine P.X. Brig off Cat. Cat."

"What's it mean, Ma?"

Susan took the paper back. "It means," she said dryly, "two runaway slaves'll be dumped here tonight by some means, that the pursuit is hot behind 'em, that we're to keep 'em until we can get 'em aboard a brig that'll be waiting off Cat Island to run 'em to Canada, and the password is 'Cat.' " She took scissors from her pocket, cut off the bottom of the bill, lit a match and burned the sliver of paper.

"But where could we hide them?" asked Hesper, suddenly a little frightened.

Susan shrugged. "Same place as we did before. No, you didn't know about it. I doubt you've sense enough now to be mixed up in a thing like this; but I've got to risk it."

"Oh Ma—I *have* sense; I'll not breathe a word."

Her mother snorted. "You'd better not. You don't want us jailed, do you? You don't want the dom copperheads setting fire to the house?"

Hesper's jaw dropped.

Susan snorted again, but now there was a twinkle in her eye. "You look as scairt as though you'd heard the Screechin' Woman. All you need is a bit of spunk, and you have got that, I should hope.

"Now listen—you know the long cupboard next the brick oven in the kitchen?"

"You mean where we keep the brooms and the old guns?"

Susan nodded impatiently. "Come, I'll show you. I reckon you've got to be told."

Hesper followed her mother back into the kitchen. It was quiet and empty as they had left it, the banjo clock ticking, the cook-stove giving off a subdued crackling. Roger's door closed.

On the walls either side of the fireplace the wide pine sheathing was darkened and glossy from the smoke of countless hearth-fires, but otherwise exactly as it had been placed by Mark Honeywood, except that a shallow cupboard had been cut through two of the planks. Susan touched the latch, and the door moved silently open on its wrought-iron snake hinges. Hesper was dumbfounded while her mother pushed the brooms and the old muskets to one side and, wedging herself into the narrow space, reached high over her head, groping for the head of a tiny iron pin which was hidden at the top and back of the closet. She pulled the pin up, releasing the two-foot wide plank, which she slid sideways to disclose a narrow opening and some wooden steps.

"Go on up," she said to Hesper; "I'll keep watch down here. Wait, take the dust-rag with you. Here—and a can of water, and some of this." She dumped gingerbread, and the remains of the sausages and fish-cakes into a wooden trencher. "We mayn't have as good a chance again to provision."

"But, Ma," whispered Hesper, "where's it go to? And what is it? I never knew . . ."

Susan twitched impatiently, then relented. "It's a pirate's hidy-hole. 'Twas built about 1700 by Lot Honeywood; he'd a sister married Davy Quelch. This Davy and his brother John pirated 'gainst the Portygees, or some such. They'd hide the loot up there. Honeywoods wasn't so domned law-abidin' in *those* days," she added with a glance towards Roger's door. "Now hurry, child."

She draped Hesper's arm with the dust-rag, added the water, trencher and a lighted candle. The girl walked nervously into the closet while Susan shut the door behind her. The flickering light showed narrow wooden steps thick with grey dust. The steps circled to the back of the central chimney, and mounted steep as a ladder to a cubicle about six feet square. It had been built from space cunningly filched from the attic and from her parents' bedroom which had once been the loft of the original house, and in a structure so full of irregularities and additions its existence had never been suspected after Moses Honeywood had added the large gambrel roofed wing to the house in 1750. Moses had left a notation about the pirate's hidy-hole amongst his private papers; but no Honeywood until Roger had bothered to look through these.

The candle trembled in Hesper's hand, she saw a lumpy shape on the floor and gave a stifled cry; but it was only a straw pallet. What if there was a ghost? Ma believed in ghosts—Old Dimond—the phantom ship —the Screechin' Woman who'd been *murdered* by pirates. So did lots of people. Her heart thumped on her ribs, and she put the candlestick on the floor. It burned calmly. An inch-wide crack, running along the ceiling, took in air from the attic. Hesper dabbed at a few cobwebs, put the food and water on the pallet, picked up the candle and retreated.

In the bright sunny kitchen Susan was mixing cornmeal for Johnny-cake, as though nothing out of the way were happening at all. She showed Hesper how to slide the false panel and drop the tiny iron pin that held it rigid. "Your Pa's gone out," she said in an acid tone, "to the station. Seems he's expecting a package of his everlastin' books from Boston. Pity *our* packages can't be handled so easy. I've been thinking, Hes, and I've made the plans. First I want you should find Johnnie."

"Johnnie Peach!" cried Hesper, her eyes shining.

"Aye, I thought you'd not object. His family's abolitionist, and he's just the boy to help with this business. We'll need a good seaman and a lad with spunk. You *can* tell *him*, but no one else, mind!"

"No, Ma," she breathed. Find Johnnie, share a great secret with him.

He'd have to notice her then. She gave an irrepressible skip, starting towards the entry where her cloak hung.

"Stop, bufflehead! That's not all. We'll need more than Johnnie. Go to Peg-leg and ask him to come here, but don't say why. I'll tell him myself."

Hesper nodded, slightly damped. Peg-leg was Susan's brother Noah Dolliber, and a stop at his house meant boring delay, for his wife was an interminable talker.

"Don't let your Aunt Mattie catch wind o' anything." She waited while Hesper nodded again. "Then go on up Gingerbread Hill, try at 'Ma'am Sociable's' and Aunty 'Crese, if they know a fiddler I can get for tonight."

"Fiddler!" cried Hesper. "Oh, Ma—you'd never mean we're going to have dancing here!" She stared at her mother with incredulous joy. Susan, a staunch church member, did not hold with frivolity of any kind. She ran the inn with stern decorum, always limiting drinks when she saw fit. And there had been no party at the "Hearth and Eagle" since the Fourth of July celebration two years ago.

"Stop teeterin' around like a chicken with the pip," she snapped, ladling the corn batter. "You needn't think I'm goin' to hold a regular tidderi-i, but since the crews'll be here and I daren't stop them comin', for they'd think it strange, there'd better be as much rumpus as possible to cover the arrival of them two packages."

"Oh, Ma—what a grand lark!" Hesper clapped her hands together, intoxicated with this succession of excitements. The secret room, find Johnnie, a fiddler and dancing.

Susan turned her bulky body and confronted her daughter squarely. "It's not a grand lark, Hesper. There be two human lives at stake. And there's danger. For them, and maybe for us, too."

The girl flushed. She'd never heard Ma use that solemn churchy voice before except once. That was the way Ma spoke so long ago at the wharf, the day they got the news that Tom and Willy were drowned.

Hesper got her cloak silently and went out the kitchen door to find Johnnie. She stood a moment in the yard, considering. It was past eight o'clock, so he'd likely be down at Appleton's Wharf by now or on the *Diana* making ready to be off tomorrow. She walked under the chestnut tree, new-leafed in tender green, and on Franklin Place turned left to the Great Harbour. The land breeze had slackened and the tide was out, so the water lay quiet; seaweed fringed the pools amongst the bare rocks on Fort Beach. There was an April softness in the salt air, that smelled of drying fish from the flakes and of oakum and tar from the wharves. There were other smells, too, less pervasive than the key odour, whiffs from privies and pigsties back of huddled houses, and a pleasanter scent of cordovan leather from the cordwainers' shops. Along Front Street the unpainted houses, weathered long ago to silver —some clinging catty corner to rock ledges, some squared with the street—presented a medley of angles and gables and gambrels, each man having built as he pleased and as he could find tenure in the scanty soil.

On the water-side, past the blacksmith's where Mr. Murchison hammered on a small anchor, and the grocers and ships' chandlers, three schooners and a square rigger from Portsmouth rode quietly at anchor in the harbour, the gaudy coloured stripes on their hulls gleaming in the sunshine. And behind them again, hugging close to the Neck, a huge Nova Scotian coaler edged up towards the coal wharves past Bartol's Head.

Hesper neared Appleton's Wharf at the foot of State Street; Swasey the fishmonger began to blow "Poko White," the Marblehead "Bankers" call, on his fish horn, thus announcing his wares, and a dozen mewing cats precipitated themselves from adjacent doorways.

Hesper picked her way briskly around the cats. The accustomed smells and sights and sounds of Marblehead made no impression on her. She was looking for Johnnie.

The wharf was teeming with busy seamen in red flannel shirts, and Guernsey frocks, and they all wore clumsy leather fishing boots made by Mr. Bessom in his wharf shop. Hesper threaded her way amongst kegs and coiled rope, passed two other schooners tied up along the wharf, the *Ceres* and the *Blue Wave*, before reaching the *Diana*.

The *Diana* was an old ship of 70 tons burden, a "pinkie" with high-peaked stern, high sides and a saucy up-tilted bowsprit. She was sluggish as an old turtle, and even her newly tarred rigging and fresh-painted blue hull and gold stripe could not disguise her air of obsolescence, but she had weathered the Great Gale of forty-six and many another, too, and her Master and crew were fond of her.

Two of the crew were toiling up the gang-plank carrying a cask of water. Hesper knew them by sight, but a sudden shyness prevented her calling to them, nor did she dare go on board without invitation. Bred as she was to the water-front, she saw that they were stowing in the hold the last of the Great General, which consisted of the salt, the water, the fuel and tackle. The Small General, which consisted of provisions, would be already on board.

She walked to the end of the dock, trying to peer into the *Diana's* square, dark portholes, when she heard an unwelcome drawl behind her. "Well, now if it isn't Fire-top! Have you come to ship with us, my lass?"

Hesper frowned and turned around. It was Nat Cubby, staring at her morosely, one foot resting on a stanchion, and his jaws languidly champing a plug of tobacco. He was twenty now and still an undersized and scrawny youth, but there was a quality in Nat which cancelled all impression of youth or smallness. He had wiry strength, the stubble of beard on his narrow jaws was heavy as a full-grown man's, and his yellowish eyes were wary and unyielding like those of an old lynx. As he contemplated Hesper, his mouth set in its perpetual slight sneer. It was a thin red scar that drew up the right half of his upper lip, but it was hard to allow for that, the resultant snarl was so in keeping with his usual manner. Nobody knew for sure how his lip had been split open; it might have been some boyish accident, but many thought it had been done by Leah, his mother, in a fit of the madness with which she had been afflicted after her husband was lost at sea. Yet Nat adored his mother, never leaving her alone when he was ashore, and she was the only person to whom he did not show a brooding malevolence.

Leah was but sixteen years older than her son, her curly hair was a glossy black, her mouth full and red as a girl's, and her magnificent dark eyes were luminous and unstained by the agonizing tears they must have shed. Strangers seeing her beside Nat might have thought them almost the same age.

"Well, what d'you want?" repeated Nat to Hesper, spitting into the water. "We want no women cluttering about the wharf at loading time."

"I came to find Johnnie Peach," said Hesper with spirit. "I've a message for him."

"You won't find him here. Likely he's gone home. I gave him leave."

"You gave him leave . . ."

The small eyes, cold as yellow glass, surveyed her without interest. "I'm mate on this ship now." He hunched a shoulder towards the *Diana*.

"Then for sure Johnnie'll be a mate soon, too," she cried hotly. "Or skipper over you," she added to herself.

Nat shrugged and shifted his tobacco to the other cheek. "Very likely he will. He's an apt seaman." You couldn't tell whether he was mocking or not, but Hesper was silenced. There'd always been a queer sort of companionship between Johnnie and Nat. Queer because as boys they'd belonged to different gangs, Johnnie a "Barnegatter," Nat a "Wharf Rat," and they'd fought each other many a time, and while everyone liked Johnnie, nobody else had a good word for Nat. Still, you couldn't tell what Nat was really like. He seemed indifferent now, remote—but you always had the feeling there was a lot going on in his head too, she thought, with sudden disquiet, remembering an argument in the taproom when Nat had sneered at all the abolitionists gathered there, and obviously from no motive but malice and the desire to annoy.

"You coming to the inn tonight?" she asked quickly. She felt herself flush and tried to look indifferent.

The yellow eyes shifted and rested on her. "I might." He took his boot off the stanchion, and walked up the gang-plank on to the *Diana*.

Lord, thought Hesper, if he should get wind of anything he'd turn us in sure. For the reward, if not just for devilry. But Johnnie'll know what to do.

She gathered her cloak around her and hurried down the wharf and along State Street. The Cubbys' house was in the middle of the block; she glanced at it and saw a slender black figure standing on the roof behind the railings. The white face was turned towards the sea, and even at that distance gave an impression of stillness and patient waiting. Hesper felt a thrill of horror; had Leah taken to standing in the "scuttle" again, as she used to day in and day out during her madness, watching for her drowned husband's ship? Hesper hurried faster, but the eerie

78

fear subsided before common sense. Leah's madness was over long ago. She had merely climbed to the scuttle to look for Nat on the wharf, so that she might know when he started home.

Hesper turned down Washington Street, and now her progress was impeded by traffic on the narrow sidewalk. Old seamen, past sailing, were wandering uptown to bask in the sun on the steps of the Town House, or on chairs outside the firehouses, and shawled women carrying wicker baskets were market-bound to the shops around Mechanic Square. Two of these, Mrs. Cloutman and Mrs. Devereux, stopped Hesper to ask her if her Ma were going to provide the cakes for the church supper at the Old North on Wednesday.

"I don't know; I guess so," said Hesper distractedly. "I'll remind her." But the women didn't yet let her pass. "What you doin' out o' school, Hes?" said Mrs. Cloutman sternly, eyeing the girl's flushed haste.

"Errand for Ma. Going to be terrible busy tonight."

"Humph," said Mrs. Cloutman unsatisfied, but Hesper Honeywood wasn't the kind to be up to mischief. Big homely girl and a good student at the Academy, she knew through her own daughter.

Hesper escaped, but only for a block when Captain Knight came bearing down on her. She bobbed her head and stood aside for him to pass, as all children must for a sea captain. But this skipper, whose ship was not sailing for the spring fare, was in no hurry.

"Mornin', child," he said. "Be'nt ye Hes Honeywood?" He rested on his brier-thorn stick, his fringe-bearded face turned towards her amiably.

"Yes, sir." She tried to edge around him, but he lifted his stick and playfully held her back. "Gr-reat stroppin' gur-rl, ye've gr-rown to. Oi moind when ye was no bigger'n a minnow, tumblin' about the wharves. Ye favour the Dollibers, Oi see, wi' all thot carrot hair."

"Yes, sir," repeated Hesper. "Please, I must be off . . ."

"Sweet-hor-rt waitin' fur ye? Ye'd best drap hobnails in the tallow pot, 'n see if he loves ye true, lass. Aye well—shove off if ye must." The captain lowered his stick. " 'Tis a stavin' spring mor-rnin', Oi can't blame ye."

Oh dear, thought Hesper, hurrying past the Old North and up the hill on Orne Street. It's getting so late—suppose Johnnie isn't home any more, suppose he's gone out in his dory.

The Peach house was set back from the street in the old section of the town called Barnegat, perched on the cliff that overlooked Little Harbour. It was a small house and quite new, being built only thirty years ago, but already its clapboards had weathered to a buff-toned silver like the older houses.

Johnnie's mother, Tamsen Peach, opened the door to Hesper. Mrs. Peach had a baby at her breast, a weanling tugging on her skirt, and the five-year-old twins scrambled on the rush-strewn kitchen floor behind her. Johnnie was the oldest of nine living children. Not a particularly large family for Marblehead.

"Well, Hessie," said Mrs. Peach, her kind rosy face breaking into a smile. " 'Tis donkey's years sence Oi've set eyes on ye. Come in and set. Oi'm bakin' the Sable cake fur Johnnie's sea chest."

"Where is Johnnie?" said Hesper so anxiously that his mother gave her a startled look. "I mean, Ma . . ." No that wasn't right, why would Ma summon Johnnie. "I wanted to say good-bye to him," she finished lamely, since Johnnie had sailed on many a fare when she hadn't seen him at all.

A smile twitched at the mother's mouth. So many girls after Johnnie, and he'd scant use for them.

"Well, ye may then," she said gently. "He's out back in the shoe-shop."

Hesper thanked her and went outdoors. The Peaches' shoe-shop stood in the backyard between the privy and the shed. It was a small wooden room lighted by two windows and warmed by a pot-bellied stove, as were all the hundred other backyard shoe-shops in Marblehead. Here the men worked during the winters and at other times when they might be in port, skiving and lasting and sewing and finishing shoes for delivery to the maufactories, the uppers having been earlier stitched and bound by the women in their kitchens during moments snatched from cookery and baby care.

Hesper heard the sound of tapping and men's voices inside, and she hesitated at the door. The shoe-shops were male sanctums like ships, where women intruded only with haste and apology. Then she heard Johnnie's easy laugh, and she knocked.

"Come in, then," called the gruff voice of Johnnie's father, Lem.

Hesper opened the door and paused, choked by the thick air. Smoke poured from the cracks of the pot-bellied stove where they were burning scraps of shoe leather, and it poured too from four white clay pipes. The warming glue-pot on the stove exhaled its own stench, and the visible air that swirled around the three cordwainers' heads was white with chalk dust.

"Why, 'tis Hessie Honeywood," said Johnnie, who had been lounging on a stool, smoking and reading the *Essex County Gazette* to the shoemakers.

Lem Peach looked up from his last. "Well—come in gur-rl, an' shet the door, ye're makin' a domned draft." He coughed long and hard, ejecting the blood-specked spittle against the stove. His face was pinched and pale, and his thin shoulders were peaked in the shoe-makers' stoop.

"Will ye set down?" said Johnnie, laughing a little and pointing to the stool he had vacated. "It's rare we have a visit from a lady."

Hesper smiled timidly and shook her head, her heart beat fast as it always did at the sight of Johnnie—his close-cropped dark hair, the thick muscles of his neck rising careless and easy from the open red flannel shirt, and his blunt white teeth grinning at her.

She glanced at Lem Peach, hunched on the cobbler's bench, and at the other two cordwainers, Barnegat men whom she did not know. "Might I speak with you a bit?" she said to Johnnie. "Are you busy?"

His father snorted. "He's not that! He's no hand for shoemaking, gr-reat clumsy loon. He's good for naught but the sea." Lem drew his sparse brows into a scowl, but a baby would have heard the pride in his voice. "Afor-re ye go out, Johnnie—hand me me 'long-stick' and a cup o' grog. Can't stop work for a minute if we're to deliver all these pairs to Porterman's on time." He took a pull from the tin cup of grog and handed it to the man on the next bench. "I mislike that Porterman," he added gloomily; "hulkin' penny-pinchin' furriner from Danvers, nor do I like his foreman neither, ever a huffin- and a dingin' at us to horry up with the consignment. We be free men here in Marblehead, not nigger slaves."

"Right you are, Pa," said Johnnie, puffing on his pipe. "Don't you let 'em boss you; cordwainers've always been their own masters, slow or fast as they willed, and where'd the manufacturers be without you—tell me that?"

The three men grunted; Lem coughed, polishing a gleaming chalk-white sole with his mahogany long-stick. "And the bostard talks of lower wages, too. As it is, we barely keep body and soul together at three dollars the case." He picked up a pig-skin bristle and waxed his thread.

"Johnnie," whispered Hesper, fearing this talk of prices and Porterman, whoever he might be, would go on for ever.

"Oh aye, aye lass," said Johnnie kindly, putting his pipe in his pocket. "Mustn't keep a lady waitin'." He made a bow, and stood aside for her to precede him into the sunlight.

"Well, Hes—what's on your mind?" He glanced with amusement at her worried face and twitched the long auburn pigtail that swung down her back. "You been filchin' your Ma's pasties again? Or, come to think on it, why be'nt you in school; 'tis very wrong to play hookey."

"Oh, Johnnie, I'm not. I'm not a child any more. It's a grave matter. We mustn't be overheard."

He chuckled. "You don't say. Well, come up Burial Hill then, the gravestones'll not listen."

He shambled along beside her, but his rolling seaman's gait was fast and, long as her legs were, she had to trot to keep up with him. Much courting took place at night on Burial Hill amongst the old graves, and more than courting too. But this April morning there was no one in sight.

They climbed the sharp hill to the highest spot by the Seamen's Monument. It commemorated many a drowned seaman, and Johnnie's uncle and Hesper's two brothers amongst them; but neither of the young people glanced at it. Johnnie squinting out to sea immediately forgot Hesper. There was one of the new clipper ships beating to wind-ward off Little Misery, Salem bound, she'd be. He shaded his eyes with his hand until he was sure of her. She was the *Flying Cloud*, for he saw the angel figurehead plain under the bowsprit. Then her Master'd be Captain Josh Cressy of Marblehead. A pretty enough craft, but over-flimsy and tender, a toy for feverish transporting of landlubbers. She'd never stand up in even a half gale off the Banks, he thought, jealous for the old *Diana*, whose masts he could see swaying gently above the shed on Appleton's Wharf in the harbour below.

"Johnnie," cried Hesper, tugging at his arm, "*please* listen to me."

He lowered his head and patted the hand on his arm. "Sorry, Hes. Out with it." He threw himself down on the bank, and pulling a grass blade began to chew.

"Johnnie, you *are* abolitionist, aren't you?" she said, abandoning all subtle approaches.

He sat up straight, his indulgent gaze sharpened to surprise. "I am. You've not inveigled me out here to start political argument?"

"No, but Ma wants your help, tonight. There's two—two packages being delivered at the inn, and we've to hide them."

He stared at her and gave a long whistle. "The Underground?" She nodded, and he drew his brows together, "Where are they to go after?"

"Canada. There's to be a big brig off Cat Island, waiting. Lucky it's the dark of the moon."

"To be sure. They're allowing for that. They always plan well."

"Then you've done this before?"

He smiled and spat out the grass. "It's often best not to question if you don't want to hear lies. Now tell me all you know about this thing."

"I know *all* about it," she said hotly. "Ma and I are doing it together; Pa wouldn't."

"So? Well, get on with it." She had his full attention at last, and he listened gravely, nodding sometimes as she told all that had happened that morning, and her mother's plans. "But," she added as she finished the account, "I'm afeared of Nat Cubby, he'll be at the inn tonight."

"Oh, he's all right," Johnnie said heartily. But he wasn't so sure. There wasn't the old free understanding between them. Nat was a bit like a cat, you never knew which way he'd jump, except it'd be to his own advantage. But Nat was smart at anything he'd turn his hand to. Johnnie didn't begrudge him the mate's berth; he'd worked hard for it. He'd be a good mate, maybe, if he didn't get one of his savage, vindictive notions when no man could make him see reason. "All the same," he said out loud, "would be best he knew nothing of this matter tonight. Run along, Hessie—get Peg-leg like your Ma said, and find a fiddler; I'll go ready my dory for his trip. Peg-leg'll have to help me row. Tide'll be racin' in against us, and there's wind makin'." He squinted at the sky.

"Yes, Johnnie," she said, turning slowly to go. Johnnie had taken over, masterful and sure, as she knew he would, but this hadn't brought him any closer to her. He hadn't looked at her once, to really see her. And why should he, she thought bitterly. I'm not so much to look at. Why didn't I take time to put on my good dress and pin my hair up.

An inkling of the girl's dejection reached Johnnie, and he thought she was frightened of the dangerous project tonight. "Hes," he said, chuckling, "d'you mind the time we stowed away on the *Balance* to fetch the salt?"

"Oh yes," she breathed, happy that he should refer to their childhood companionship.

"You were a plucky one. Got the makin' of a seaman, too, shouldn't wonder." Her eyes shone, dazzled by this highest praise, and then Johnnie spoiled it. "It's mortal shame you're only a girl."

She put her lips tight together and walked away. Johnnie, after a moment's surprise, forgot about her and started down the hill towards Little Harbour and his new dory.

Hesper continued in the other direction, along Beacon Street to Dolliber's Cove and Peg-leg's neat cottage. She was startled to find her uncle wrapped in a red blanket and lying propped up on a bench in his yard. Peg-leg, for all the strapped-on wooden stump that served him for left leg and despite his increasing plumpness, was nimble as a jack-rabbit. He still went out dory fishing in the bay, and he was a great gardener. From May to September his little yard bloomed with daffodils or cinnamon roses, moss pinks or asters.

"Why Peg-leg," cried Hesper, pushing open the gate and hurrying up to the red cocoon on the bench, "whatever's the matter?"

The round face above the fringe of sandy beard surveyed her sourly. "Where's yore manners, chit? Yore Grand-sir Dolliber hear ye callin' me thot, he'd a guv ye a stroppin', he would. Susan'd ought to raise ye better."

"I'm sorry, Uncle Noah," said Hesper, accurately deducing great stress from this unusual cantankerousness. Half the town had nicknames everybody used, and Peg-leg never minded his. "Ma wanted to see you at the inn, right-away."

"Well, she won't then. Nor see me at all, lessen she comes here. Oi'm thot kinked up wi' t' rheumatiz Oi wouldn't budge fur Old Nick hisself."

"I'm sorry," said Hesper again. So Peg-leg wouldn't be any use to Johnnie tonight; who then could he get to help him? Well, he'd make another plan, Johnnie was never at a loss; but . . . a blinding and thrilling idea struck her. She straightened her strong young shoulders. If only she could persuade him. . . .

Her uncle saw the sudden brightening of her face and was naturally annoyed.

"Me pains're far worser now then after the God-domned shark bit me leg off," he said peevishly, scowling at her.

"It's mortal shame—Peg—Uncle Noah. Have you tried the goose-grease?" She was in a fever to be off on the rest of her errand, and dismayed to see her aunt come bustling through the door into the yard.

"Who're ye a gabbin' with, Noah. Oh, I see 'tis Hessie. How be ye, child, an' how's your Ma and Pa? He's real grouty wi' t' rheumatics." She jerked her double chins in the direction of her husband. "Oi'm cookin' him up a garney stew. Me Father-r useter say there was naught like tongues and sounds and fins well seethed in a bit o' broth fur strenthenin' the belly. D'ye member me Pa, Hessie? Master o' the *Rebecca* he was?" The insistent babbling voice paused an instant.

"Oh yes, Aunt Mattie, I do," cried Hesper with complete untruth; "I must be—"

"Nay, to be sure ye don't," went on her aunt, whose pauses were always for breath and not for response. "Ye wasn't barn yet when he died. An' speakin' o' dying—does yore Ma know Puff-ball Thompson expired yester-e'en. Oi was there, an' 'twas the drink did her in, wi'out doubt, fur she stank loike a dram-shop. But maybe we've no cause to blame her fur drownin' her troubles, when ye think there's her brat Cassie, eight months gone by Rob Nicholls and him China bound out o' Salem, an' not loike to wed her even—"

"Mattie!" Peg-leg opened his eyes. "Ye forget yore hearer." His wife was no way discomfited. "Well, Oi should hope Hessie's old enough to take warnin' from the sins o' others, an' Cassie's not the only one either. Oi have grave doubts about . . ." The acrid odour of scorching fish swirled out the kitchen door. Mattie sniffed reluctantly and said, "Crimmy—there's me garney a-catchin' itself. Wait, Hes—Oi'll be back directly." But Hesper did not wait.

As she climbed the narrow sharp lane up Gingerbread Hill, she briefly considered Aunt Mattie's last remarks. What had Cassie and Rob Nicholls done exactly, that Cassie should be "eight months gone." That it was something shameful and to do with a baby, Hesper understood. But people had babies after they were married, not before. Sows and bitches could be "eight *weeks* gone" not months—there was perhaps some connexion, but for Hesper not a convincing one. She couldn't ask Ma, who'd slapped her once for mentioning the old sow's tits. The girls at school were always whispering and giggling in corners; they might know, but she had no intimate friend she cared to ask. Her interest lagged and reverted to Johnnie and the adventure tonight.

She reached the top of the hill by Black Joe's Pond, and hesitated in the lane between the two rival taverns. The Widow Bowen, "Ma'am Sociable," lived in one, and "Aunt 'Crese" lived in the other. They both ran cent shops, and sold election cakes, ginger-bread and Gibraltars, as well as grog. Both women were shrewd and easy-going, both held frolics and jigs and reels and penny-pitching contests, in an endeavour to lure customers away from each other's establishments. "Ma'am Sociable" was a spry little elf of a woman with faded flaxen hair; "Aunt 'Crese" was fat and dark as soot, the widow of "Black Joe," who had been a free negro and fought in the Revolution. Marbleheaders in search of gaiety patronized them quite impartially.

At Hesper's approach the flock of white geese on the pond set up a raucous cackling and honking. The Widow Bowen flew out the door and down her stone steps. "Come in, come in, dearie. Your Ma send ye fur my rose water? I've got a bottle or so left." Over Hesper's auburn head she saw Aunt 'Crese waddle through her own doorway, and she raised her voice to a high wheedle. "I've got fresh gingerbread-nuts, or some mighty pretty ribbons; you've pennies with you, haven't you?"

"Only two," said Hesper, fumbling in her pinafore pocket. Maybe a red ribbon tied into a bow at the neck of her best dress for tonight. . . .

Aunt 'Crese reached the lane and her thick molasses voice flowed over them. "Mornin' young lady—ah got some tasty nice pep'mint drops today, some purty pitcher cyards too, theyse got li'l pink hearts on 'em an' li'l gol' doves, sho you want to see 'em." She ignored her rival and bestowed on the girl a dazzling smile.

Hesper, flanked by the small insistent white woman in a sun-bonnet and the large determined black one in a yellow turban, suddenly giggled. "I didn't really come to buy. Ma wants to know, will you send her a fiddler for tonight?"

Both women stopped looking persuasive, and drew together in a momentary bond of caution against outside competition.

"What's Mrs. Honeywood want a fiddler for?" snapped Widow Bowen; "she never has jamborees at her inn."

"Well, she's holding a farewell for the men on the *Diana* and the *Ceres*; thought they'd like maybe to dance a bit," said Hesper pacifically.

"I'm holdin' a frolic myself," snapped Widow Bowen, who had just thought of it. "I'll need Pipin' Willy here."

"Yo' kin have Ambrose," said Aunt 'Crese, who had drawn back again and was examining Hesper, and referring to one of her grandsons. "Ah expecs yo' Ma'll pay well? Ev'body know Ambrose 'es the bes' fiddler in Essex County."

The Widow Bowen sniffed, shrugged her shoulders, and retreated. Those Honeywoods, uppity they were, hardly give you the time o' day. Let 'em try to liven up their stuffy old inn, that moony ink-stained Roger, and Susan Dolliber glum as a haddock—they'd not get far. She slammed her front door.

"Thanks, Aunt 'Crese," said Hesper. "Could Ambrose be there at seven?"

The old negress nodded; her yellowed veiny eyeballs rolled and focused keenly on the girl's face. "Yo' got su'thin' on yo' min', chile. I can see it plain."

"Oh no, I haven't," said Hesper quickly, but the old woman put two fat black hands on her shoulders and held fast. "Wait, chile, I can read a powerful lot in yo' face. Yo're to go through a heap o' livin'."

Hesper tried to back away. All morning people had been detaining her, and the old woman's breath was fetid.

Aunt 'Crese's gaze rolled inward—her purplish lips stuck out. "Le' me tell yo' fortune, chile. Yo' got two coppers ain't yo'?"

Hesper nodded. "But—"

One black hand slid down to her arm, and Aunt 'Crese pulled Hesper into her little taven. It was dark inside; from the smoke-blackened rafters there dangled hams, bunches of dried herbs and strings of corn ears. Next to the rum keg there was a glass case containing rusty pins, a spool of thread, faded picture cards, and a cracked dish of miscellaneous taffy balls, peppermint drops and Gibraltars, all filmed with dust. This was the cent shop. One of the grandsons, a lanky, bullet-headed young negro, sprawled on a pile of corn-husks near the fire, snoring fitfully. His grandmother stepped over his legs and Hesper followed. Her un-willingness had given place to interest. She'd heard that Aunt 'Crese told fortunes when the fit struck her. But Charity Trevercombe and Nellie Higgins had sneaked out here once after dark, and Aunt 'Crese hadn't told them any fortune at all; she'd made them spend all their coppers on mouldy candy they didn't want.

"Set down," ordered Aunt 'Crese, pointing at a sticky bench spotted with candle grease. Hesper did so gingerly, and the old woman pulled a lean pack of dirty playing cards from a niche under the tavern trestle.

"Cut with yo' left hand." Hesper imitated the other's gesture, staring curiously at the cards, and suffused by an agreeable feeling of excitement and guilt. She'd never seen playing cards before; Ma wouldn't allow the devil's playthings in the house.

"Make a wish." Instantly Hesper thought "Johnnie," and as instantly suppressed it; she ought to wish for something noble and unselfish—like the success of the venture tonight.

Aunt 'Crese shuffled and slapped the cards on the table. Outside on the pond the geese quacked incessantly. The young negro snored by the hearth. These were comforting noises; nor was there anything eerie about the old negress in her grimy yellow turban, even when she began to speak and her voice had gone high and thin, drifting through her pendulous lips and scarcely moving them. "Yo' goin' ter see a heap o' trouble, chile. Heart-break, heart-break. Yo'll tink it won't mend, but Life's got a hull lot up her sleeve for you. It'll mend, an' yo'll fin' out how many ways a woman's heart can break."

Hesper drew in her breath. "I don't want to hear things like that. I don't believe you, anyway."

The thin sing-song continued unheeding. "Yo'll know three kin's o' lovin'. They's three men here in yore life."

"Three?" cried Hesper incredulously, relaxing again. This was the sort of thing a fortune should tell. "Will I get—get married?"

But Aunt 'Crese stared at the cluttered cards and heeded nothing else. "There's fire aroun' yo', fire in yore hair, fire in yore heart, fire that makes a beautyness, an' real fire fearsome in the night. An' there's water too. The ocean's salt's in yore blood. Yo' cain't live without it."

What rubbish, thought Hesper, and she looked surreptitiously around the tavern for a clock.

The old woman stooped closer over the cards. "Ah see yo' scribblin' away, pen on paper, puttin' down words . . . puttin' down words."

Hesper brightened. That was her secret ambition, poetry like Pa. Like Mrs. Hemans or Mrs. Sigourney. She had a pansy album half filled with little verses.

"All them words won't do yo' no good," said Aunt 'Crese with contempt. "No good at all. Yo' want things too hard. Always hankerin' an' a-ravenin' after su'thin'. Yo' can't help it, ah reckon, but yo' should listen to the house."

The girl sighed. "I can't listen to a house," she said crossly.

"It's yore home—an' it's powerful wise effen yo'll listen to it, yo' kin hear the Words o' God through it."

"I don't see how," cried Hesper, shocked at this blasphemy. "Listen, I've got to go, Aunt 'Crese, and you haven't even told me about my wish."

The old woman waggled her head, she poked at a red-spotted card. Her voice dropped from the high whine. "Yo'll get yore love-wish, chile, but someplace there's heart-break. Heart-break," she repeated with solemn unction. She spattered the cards into a circle, heaved herself to her feet, staring at Hesper with a blend of malice and pity. "That's yo' fortune. Gi' me the two coppers."

"But, you didn't tell me anything, really." Hesper's hot hand clutched the two coppers in her pocket. One was for the Sabbath collection and the other was her weekly allowance. She felt cheated and disgruntled. Heart-break. Fire and water. Listen to the house. Three men when all she wanted was Johnnie. Get your wish—but . . .

"Ah tole yo' plenty," said Aunt 'Crese. "Ah tole yo' de truf." She drew herself up sharply until she towered over Hesper, and the shiny face went hard like black marble. "Yo' tink ah cain't see things others cain't. Yo' tink ah don't know what's hidden in the secret heart?" The fat good-natured Aunt 'Crese had become an outraged priestess. "Yo' tink ah don't know what yore up to tonight? Why yo' want Ambrose an' his fiddlin'?"

Hesper's mouth dropped open. What'll I say? Does she really know? Can she read my thoughts? Or is she part of the Underground too?

Aunt 'Crese watched her through slitted eyes and gave a throaty chuckle. She held out her thick pinkish palm, and Hesper slowly dropped the coppers into it. Aunt 'Crese tucked them in her turban, where they jingled with other coins on the grizzled wool. "Run along, chile. Ah don't meddle with nobody, an' nobody meddles with me. Run along."

Hesper nodded uncertainly and obeyed. As she walked down Gingerbread Lane, she felt a little like crying. Her two coppers were gone, and there'd be a scene with Ma about the one for the collection. The fortune had been horrid, queer and vague, and Aunt 'Crese had been horrid, queer and vague, too. How did one learn to take people, not to feel lost and inadequate when they suddenly acted different from what one expected? Like Peg-leg this morning, too. She'd never known he could be so cross. Hesper had always lived in a childish world of certainties, of black and white, and she felt rebellion and resultant helplessness at the first dim adult perception that many things must be endured without certainty. Take Aunt 'Crese, was she good or bad, did she guess or know about the Underground, or were her words just a lucky hit? Serves me right for dawdling and listening to that silly fortune.

She ran down Orne Street as distant church bells bonged twelve times. Lord, dinner'd be on, and Ma frantic to know the result of the errands. Hesper cut left between the houses and scrambled down to the Little Harbour Beach. Above high-water mark on the shingle and in the adjacent field fishermen tended the semi-circle of fish-flakes, the slatted wooden frames on which the cod splits, glittering with salt crystals, dried in the April sun. Hesper looked for Johnnie's green dory amongst the dozen boats drawn up on the beach, but it was not there. She hurried off the beach, across a lane and into the Honeywood lot, in back of the inn. Here there were four apple trees, remnant of Moses Honywood's fine orchard. Here, too, was Susan's herb patch and vegetable garden, where old "Looney" Hodge was hoeing, his vacant, half-witted face drooping over the stony soil with mournful patience. Since Roger never lent a hand, Susan hired Looney to help with the rougher chores. He slept in the barn above the pigsty and the empty stable, where the rare inn guests who did not come on foot from the station, or by water, might shelter a horse and buggy.

To her great relief she found her father alone in the kitchen. He sat at the scarred oak table, with his dinner of salt pork and pickled beets still untouched on the pewter plate before him, and a book propped up against the mug of coffee. He looked up, smiling as his girl flew into the kitchen, throwing her cape on the entry hook, patting her ruffled hair and casting a quick glance around for her mother.

"Hail, radiant daughter of an April morn," he said with the affectionate playfulness he never showed to anyone else. "Sit down, my dear, I want to read you some magnificent lines." He indicated the book before him. "One of Horace's Odes—translated by Dryden. It well expresses what I—I'm trying to instil into my own poem."

She heard the uncertainty and yet the pride in his voice, and she put her hand on his thin alpaca-covered shoulder. "Not now, Pa," she said, half smiling, half exasperated. "Where's Ma?"

"In the taproom or the parlour, I believe—making some sort of a to-do." He compressed his mouth, and frowned again through his spectacles.

"Descended from an ancient line . . ." Ah, Hesper was too young to know the subtle comfort of that, but she might have listened. He turned the page to the last stanza, reading to himself:

> "For me secure from Fortune's blows,
> Secure of what I cannot lose,
> In my small pinnace I can sail
> Contemning all the blustering roar;
> And running with a merry gale,
> With friendly stars my safety seek,
> Within some little winding creek,
> And see the storm from shore."

That was the way to take life, in contemplation and serenity.

"Eat your dinner, Pa, do," said Hesper coaxingly, seeing that she had hurt him. She nudged his full plate. "I'd love to hear the poem tomorrow."

Susan came bustling into the kitchen. "So you're back, Miss," she said, scowling at Hesper in a preoccupied way; her broad freckled face was flushed from the exertion of cleaning the always immaculate parlour and moving furniture out of the way for tonight's celebration. "My God, Roger, you're that gormy at your vittles, I'm like to go mad. Have you not enough reading shut up in your room all day? Step to the buttery," she added under her breath to Hesper.

She thrust a cheese-cloth into the girl's hands and took one herself, and they both wrung water from the waiting pats of butter, while Hesper gave a whispered account of her morning, deleting, of course the fortune-telling episode.

"So Peg-leg's out, we must trust to Johnnie alone," Susan said, shaking her head, "I daren't trust anyone else. The baker boy told me there

88

was a big nigger hunt in Lynn last night. The slave-catcher might come here next."

Hesper squeezed the butter until it jutted in ridges between her fingers. "Ma, I can row. I could help Johnnie."

"Rubbish. You'll do nothin' of the sort. No, hold your tongue; I've got enough to fret me without your buffleheaded notions."

Hesper turned her back on her mother, hot mutinous tears flew to her eyes. No uncertainties about Ma, anyway. She always said No.

The knocker on the side door between the taproom and the kitchen resounded with two heavy raps. Susan's hand paused, she put the butter in its crock. "Who's that, I wonder?" she said slowly. "Not a regular customer, or he'd've walked in." She wiped her hands on her apron. "Well, there's naught yet for anyone to find." She gave her grim chuckle and pushed past her daughter. Hesper dabbed at her eyes with the buttery cheese-cloth and followed.

She heard a deep deliberate voice say, "Mrs. Honeywood? May I speak with you a moment?" And knew from the enunciation it was no Marbleheader. Her mother answered, "In the kitchen then, sir. We're expecting some of the men off the ships tonight, and the parlour's at sixes and sevens."

A very tall and heavy-set man entered the room after Susan; he was dressed in frock-coat and striped silk waistcoat, across which a massive gold-link watch-chain ran from pocket to pocket. He held a glossy beaver top-hat politely in his hand; there was a big dent in the top of the hat. His hair, clipped short and square above his ears, was of so light a flaxen colour that it almost seemed white, and made him appear older than his twenty-six years.

Roger looked up in surprise, as the stranger entered saying, "Good day, sir. I'm sorry to disturb you. My name is Amos Porterman. I now own the old Allen shoe manufactory on School Street."

"Oh, do you indeed, sir?" answered Roger with vague hospitality and not the slightest interest. "Will you sit down?" He glanced for help to his wife, a trifle surprised at her silence and a certain wariness in her bearing.

Hesper and Susan were both more enlightened than Roger by the stranger's identification of himself. Hesper thought, with immediate antagonism, Oh, it's that dreadful shoeman from Danvers Johnnie's father was talking about. What nasty cold blue eyes he has, and what's he want butting in here? Surely, Ma'd give him short-shrift.

But Susan, though she sat down when Mr. Porterman did, said nothing. She sat waiting. This, then, was the foreigner who'd bought up the Allen factory last Fall, when Mr. Allen and all the other shoemen in town, except Bassett, went bankrupt in the panic. This big young man looked honest and open enough, but you never knew. The shoe manufactories had a large trade with the South, and many of them were copperheads.

Amos Porterman was discomfited but not surprised by his reception. He'd met nothing but varying shades of hostility all the months he'd been coming to Marblehead. "I came today, ma'am"—he turned back to Susan—"because I've been told you keep a very fine inn."

"Well . . ." said Susan. She continued to regard him steadily. He had very bushy blond eyebrows, and when he drew them together, as he did now, they gave to his blue eyes a quizzical expression, mitigating the frown. "Well, ma'am, now I've bought a factory here, I must spend some time in Marblehead to look after it. I'm not comfortable at the hotel, and I thought I'd take a room with you."

Hesper made an involuntary gesture, and said "Oh no" under her breath. Amos heard it and was annoyed. He gave her a quick glance. Unmannerly red-headed chit, gawky and untidy. Surely that was a dab of butter on her cheek? And what right had those greenish eyes to stare at him from under those peculiar dark eyebrows with such a frank dislike.

"I've no rooms just now, Mr. Porterman," said Susan after a pause. "I seldom let 'em out, anyhow, except to drummers for a night. I've all I can do with the taproom."

"You mean," snapped Amos, all at once losing his temper, "that you don't want me here! You confounded Marbleheaders . . . My factory's giving work to your folk who need it. I don't see why you . . ." He clenched his big hand and shut his mouth with a snap, thinking of his walk here down Washington Street. A gang of small boys had thrown stones at him from ambush behind the Town House, yelling "Stone him outa town! Squael the dor-rty furriner!"

To Hesper and Roger's amazement no less than Amos's, Susan suddenly laughed. "Maybe we be a mite hard on foreigners, and maybe some of us like the old ways best when we didn't have to depend on shoes for work; the sea did it all. But times change, and I don't know as I blame you for being grouty."

Why, Ma likes him, thought Hesper dumbfounded. Ma always liked a bit of spunk and temper in a man, but a *shoeman*—from Danvers, bad as Salem and so big and sleek and fancy-clothed. Why, he actually smelled of bay-rum, she thought, sniffing, instead of fish and rum, as a man should.

"Well, Ma'am, I'll be going," said Amos, only slightly mollified by Susan's speech. "Sorry to trouble you folks." He bent his big body in a stiff bow.

"You want a place to board," said Susan, who had made up her mind that this man had come here with no sinister intent. "You might try Mrs. Leah Cubby on State Street. She takes roomers."

"Oh, really!" Amos turned from the door, grateful for any softening. The manufactory did well, but aside from his foreman he had no one to talk to in Marblehead. These people with their peculiar words and rough burring dialect kept so tightly to themselves on their rocky promontory, you'd have thought them living in a fortress. Opposition always roused his dander, and he'd have moved here altogether, forced them to accept him, if it weren't for Lily Rose.

"Cubby's an odd name," he said at random, conversationally.

At this Mr. Honeywood raised his head from the book he was reading and spoke in the tone of a tolerant school-master. "It's derived from Cubier, a Guernsey name. We have many such here, though not quite as old as the English stock, like mine." He bent his head again.

"Oh," said Amos. Queer Dick, this Honeywood was, with his ink-stained fingers and his spectacles and long, thin, baldish head. Pride of family evidently. Well, you met that in Danvers, too, and damn silly it was.

"You're married, a'nt you, Mr. Porterman?" said Susan, glancing at his wide gold wedding-band. She had been thinking that Leah was a mighty handsome woman.

"Yes, I am. But my wife is an invalid. She stays at our home in Danvers." Lily Rose and her lacy pink negligées, her medicine bottles and her strained, sweet smiles. Must remember to buy her a present before I go home.

"Well, will you try the Widow Cubby's?" said Susan sharply, and Hesper was relieved to hear her mother's normal impatience returned. This stranger was interrupting everything, holding up the preparations for tonight, standing there like a hulk, not sense enough to go. Let him go to Leah's, or back to the hotel, or sleep on the wharves, so long as he got out of here. A bore he was, and patronizing too. She hadn't missed the disdainful look he cast around the kitchen when he came in.

And in this she was quite right. After Amos had bowed himself out, he walked along Front toward State Street to interview the Widow Cubby, and he thought with pity and contempt of the Honeywoods. Older than the Ark, that house; wouldn't you think they'd make shift somehow to get some new furniture, and at least cover the rough plank flooring with some decent oil-cloth? Shiftless, run to seed, except perhaps the mother. She had a briskness and toughness about her that appealed to him. That Honeywood, no gumption, well educated obviously and done nothing about it. Amos thought of his own career. Father came to Danvers about 1818. From where—New York, New Jersey? Amos didn't remember, had never been interested. Married a Scotch hired girl, set up a tannery, did well. Died worth ten thousand. And I'm going to do a sight better than that. I know shoes from the hides up, and I know manufacturing. When I die I'll leave a hundred thousand and—more. Leave it to whom? He sighed. If Lily Rose would only get stronger. Maybe the sea air would help if he could only persuade her to move here. Could a tart, sensible woman like Mrs. Honeywood make Lily Rose pull herself together? He thought again of the curious antiquated inn, smelling of sea air and smoke, of the dominating rough-voiced wife, and the vague bookworm of a husband, wondering if all Marbleheaders were as strange. Of Hesper he did not think at all.

CHAPTER FOUR

By six o'clock the guests, having finished their supper, began to arrive at the "Hearth and Eagle" for the evening's frolic. The fishermen off the *Ceres* and the *Diana* were spruced up in their best double-breasted grey flannel shirts, knitted "Gansey" jackets and flowing black silk ties, their oiled rubber boots discarded tonight for shiny black brogans made in their own little cordwainer shops. Those men who had wives brought them of course, for this was a social gathering, and Susan had extended invitations through little Benjie, the grocer's boy.

Hesper, upstairs in her bedroom, heard the frequent tinkle of the bell that hung over the taproom door, and tried to hurry.

Her best dress was a dark-blue poplin, made over from one of her mother's. It was trimmed, on the skirt and sleeves, with rows of Turkey red rick-rack, bought cheap by Susan from a pedlar. Hesper, never much aware of clothes, had been satisfied with the dress. Now she wasn't so sure. It didn't seem to fit just right, tight across the bust and bunchy on one shoulder. She loathed sewing, always impatient to get outdoors or back to the book she was reading, but now she wished that she had paid more attention to the pattern her mother had cut for her. Charity Trevercombe was coming tonight, and she always wore lovely dresses.

Her last anxious look into the mirror ended in dissatisfaction as usual. She had tried her hair in three different ways, determined that no matter what Ma said, she would not wear it in a long pig-tail like a little girl. The flamboyant masses of fiery tendrils refused to conform. They wouldn't sleek down over her ears from a centre parting, and they wouldn't make a neat knot on the nape of her neck. She finally coiled the heavy braid around her head, skewering it with slippery bone hair-pins, and the result made her scalp ache. She put on her only jewel, a mourning brooch, onyx and silver, inherited from Gran, and went nervously downstairs.

Her father met her in the hall. Roger, too, had taken unusual pains with his appearance, and his antique and seedy frock-coat was redeemed by a snowy stock and old-fashioned, gold-button waistcoat. Although in general he never mingled with the inn's customers, this was different. This farewell to the crews was part of tradition. He had no intention of staying long amongst the company nor much interest in any of them, but he wandered from group to group, greeting them with vague benevolence, and pleased to see his house in gala mood. The oldest house in Marblehead, and certainly the finest, he thought complacently, now that its erstwhile rivals, "King Hooper's" house and the Lee Mansion, had deteriorated from their last-century glories and been converted to commercial purposes—a dry-goods store and a bank.

Susan had thrown open all the "New" wing tonight, he was delighted to see. He wandered through the great hall with its fluted and white-painted panelling, illumined by candles in gilded sconces. He gazed with deep pleasure at the elaborate carved stairway, its newel-post like a thick, white icicle. The staircase led up to the four large bedrooms that were never used except by the infrequent overnight guests.

Susan had even opened the small second parlour across the hall from the main entrance, though it was but inadequately furnished, and she kept it as a box-room.

Roger returned from his prowl of inspection and drifted up to the two sea captains, Caswell from the *Ceres* and Lane of the *Diana*, who stood chatting together near the punch-bowl in the tap-room.

"Good evening, sirs, good evening," Roger said heartily. "You're most welcome, and your men, too. Have you sampled the punch? Susan took pains with it, I know." The refreshments were on the house tonight, so Susan had closed the bar and provided a five-gallon tub filled with rum punch.

The two Banks skippers had each been boasting of the merits of his own schooner, the smartness of his particular crew and the unprecedented number of quintals of cod he was sure to catch. Now they broke off and turned politely to their host.

"Why sure, Rahger-r," said Captain Lane, who had sat on the same bench with him forty-five years ago in the little Orne Street school-house. "Punch is a stavin' foine dr-rink, war-rms a mon's belly an' per-rks his sperrits."

"It is Lot Honeywood's recipe—Moses' father," said Roger gratified, never doubting that his listeners would know which ancestor he referred to, as indeed they did in a general way. Most of the old Marble-headers knew the names of each other's grand-sirs and great grand-sirs, and they shared many in common.

"Lot wrote the punch recipe down up there," continued Roger, pointing to some lines of crooked letters which ran along the great "summer" beam athwart the taproom, and, quite oblivious to his hearers' interest, proceeded to recite:

> " 'Punch
> *The name consists of letters five,*
> *By five ingredients 'tis kept alive;*
> *To purest water sugar must be joined,*
> *With these the greatful lemon is combined.*
> *When now these three are mixed with care*
> *Then added be of spirit a good share,*
> *And that you may the drink quite perfect see*
> *Atop the musky nut must grated be.'*

And that's exactly how it's made here to this day a hundred and fifty years later," he finished with pride.

Hesper heard this from her seat on a hassock in the big parlour near her mother, and was touched and amused. Poor Pa, he didn't know Ma didn't make the punch that way at all. She used tea instead of water and molasses instead of sugar, and a whole bottle of port wine as well as the rum. But Pa didn't know lots of things, and he didn't see that he'd checked all the easy talk there'd been amongst the seamen. The two skippers and those of their men who had arrived stood now in a stiff row waiting for his precise voice to stop.

She sighed. He doesn't know how to get on with people, and I guess

I don't either. But there wasn't anything for her to do right now, except wait. It wasn't seemly for her to go into the taproom where the men were, until the dancing began, and, anyway, Johnnie hadn't come yet. She kept watching through the door. So she sat bleakly on her hassock and listened to her mother and Mrs. Cap'n Lane discuss the Church Supper and the Ladies' Fancy Work Sale.

Susan and Mrs. Lane sat upon the long horsehair sofa, their sombre bombazine skirts arranged in decorous folds, their voices subdued as befitted the dignity of the seldom-opened parlour.

This large square parlour was Susan's great pride and compensation for the rest of the house. The parlour was quite up-to-date and elegant. None of its furnishings was earlier than Moses Honeywood's time, and of those only the French wall-paper, with its hunting scenes in faded maroon, the spinet and the Biblical tiles around the fireplace. The what-not, loaded with shell-work, scrimshaw and china figures, had been acquired by Roger's father, as had the horsehair chairs and sofa; while the bright green and cabbage-rose carpeting Susan had scrimped to buy herself. There was a centre table with a fringed yellow plush throw, and on top of that the Bible and the Family Album flanking a large oil-lamp with a white-globe chimney frosted in ferns. There were candles, too, in sconces along the wall and in china candlesticks on the mantelpiece. Though Susan always preferred lamps when possible—candles dripped wax and made a mess.

At a quarter of seven, Charity Trevercombe arrived with her mother. They entered by the formal front door on the harbour side of Moses' wing, and Hesper, hurrying to greet them, felt a new despondency. Charity wore a dress of ruffled cherry-coloured taffeta; her chestnut hair fell over her shoulders in soft perfect ringlets, from her ears dangled little gold ear-rings shaped like butterflies, and she looked extraordinarily pretty.

Nor could Hesper help seeing the quiver of attention that ran through the men in the taproom, a sort of kindling; even old Cap'n Lane patted his tie and shifted position at the punch-bowl so he could watch the little cherry-coloured figure.

"Oh, Hessie—isn't this a lark!" trilled Charity, flitting around the parlour and settling as near the men as she dared. "I do love dancing. What other girls are coming?"

"Why, I guess Nellie Higgins and Bessie Bowen, and I think Ma asked the Selmans and the Picketts." She broke off, staring into the taproom.

"There's Johnnie Peach!" cried Charity. "My, he looks almost handsome. Haven't seen him in ages. Guess he'll ask me for the first reel."

She dimpled and fluttered her eyelashes as Johnnie walked into the parlour, but though he grinned at the girls and made them a mock salute, he went past them to the horsehair sofa. "Evenin', ma'ams," he said, bowing to Susan, Mrs. Cap'n Lane and Mrs. Trevercombe. "Fine night for a party. It's blowin' up a bit outside though. Wind's shifted."

Hesper, watching and straining to hear, saw her mother's eyes meet

Johnnie's for a thoughtful second. "I hope 't won't blow hard enough to hold you in the harbour—tomorrow." The pause before the last word was obvious only to Hesper and Johnnie.

"Why no, ma'am; I don't doubt we'll get out."

Mrs. Lane bridled; after all, her husband was Master of the *Diana* and Johnnie only one of the crew. "That's for Cap'n Lane to say—John Peach. He'll do as he thinks best."

"Yes'um," said Johnnie submissively. Mrs. Trevercombe rearranged her bonnet strings and looked bored. Johnnie Peach was a nice enough boy for a fisherman, but she hadn't missed her daughter's flutters and dimplings as he came in. She doubted the wisdom of letting Charity come tonight, not likely to meet any of the few really eligible young men in Marblehead.

Now the two large rooms began to fill. Nellie Higgins and Bessie Bowen arrived together with their families; then the Selmans and the Picketts from up Franklin Street. The men, having fortified themselves, temporarily abandoned the punch-bowl and mingled with the ladies. Ambrose, the fiddler, arrived promptly at seven, was stationed on a box in a corner of the taproom, where he set up a premonitory squeaking and scraping, upon which Roger, feeling that he need do no more in the interests of hospitality, vanished to his study.

The girls clustered together in the parlour by the spinet, trying to look unconscious as the young seamen began to edge towards them.

"Here he comes," whispered Charity complacently, and referring to Johnnie, of course. But Johnnie looked right over her head to Hesper, who had drawn back to the wall, miserably conscious of her height and the inadequacies of her blue poplin.

"Come on, Hes," said Johnnie, holding out his hand, "we'll start 'em off."

Charity said "Oh" under her breath, tossed her head, and accepted Willy Bowen, who was mate on the *Ceres*. Hesper found herself still clinging to Johnnie's square brown hand, and dropped it with a furious blush. "I don't know many steps," she murmured, "I—"

"It doesn't matter, no more do I. But I wanted a word with you."

They took their positions at the head of the set, and while the other couples formed beside them, Johnnie muttered out of the corner of his mouth, "Where's Peg-leg?"

"Sick. Couldn't come," she whispered back.

Johnnie frowned, while he seized her hands and they galloped down the aisle of jigging, clapping young bodies. He said, "This job'll take a bit of doin'. Is your Ma keepin' watch?"

She nodded, for Susan had seated herself in the parlour so that she might see unobtrusively through the west window which overlooked the street. "'Tisn't time yet." And I wish it never would be, Hesper thought.

This business tonight now seemed to her an unwelcome and foolish interruption. She was happy, dancing with Johnnie, leading the set and dancing better than she had hoped to. The music was exciting—"Money Musk," "Sir Roger de Coverley." Ambrose was a good fiddler, the round mellow notes winged from his fiddle and filled the old taproom with the essence of gaiety. The light from a dozen candles flickered on smiling faces, the oak planks, glistening with a fresh coat of bees-wax, resounded under stamping, exuberant feet. Later there'd be forfeits—maybe Johnnie'd still be her partner, and if the forfeit was a kiss. . . .

She completed a left and right around the circle, stood again before him, panting a little—her eyes shining, but Johnnie didn't see her. He stared past her towards the entry, his eyes slightly narrowed, his lips tight. She followed his gaze and saw Nat Cubby with a strange man. Oh dear, she thought, for Johnnie muttered and dropped out of the dancing; she tagged along behind him as he sauntered up to the newcomers. "I was wonderin' if you was comin' tonight," he said to Nat, and raised his eyebrows towards the stranger.

This was a lanky man with a black moustache, a flowered waistcoat, grey pantaloons, and a broad silk belt from which protruded the handle of a revolver. "Good evening," the stranger said easily; "hope I'm not intruding. Happened to have a bit of business in Marblehead tonight. Ran into my young friend here on the pier; asked him where I could find a little drink, so he brought me along." The black moustache lifted in an ingratiating smile.

"Taproom's closed to the public," said a sharp voice. Susan had squeezed past the dancers, and she stood behind Hesper and Johnnie, arms folded across her black silk bosom.

"Why, I'm sorry for that, ma'am," drawled the stranger, bowing to her; "but you'd not turn away a weary traveller, would you? It's been a long journey, first and last—from Carolina I started. But there's been many a stop since." He smiled again. "At Swansea," he added reflectively; "at Medford—and last night at Lynn. You see, ma'am, you might say I've been searching for something."

No muscle moved in Susan's broad freckled face as she heard the insinuating drawl tick off the nearest stations on the "Underground." Hesper, for a moment not understanding, felt Johnnie beside her take a quick breath. Why it's a slave-catcher, she thought, suddenly enlightened. She stared at the revolver. The stranger gently buttoned up his coat. Nat leaned against the wall, watching all of them from his sardonic yellowish eyes, his mouth lifted in the lifeless smile.

The music stopped with a flourish of twirling dancers and a burst of clapping.

"You're welcome to a mug o' punch," said Susan, "since you've come so far and Nat brought you, but—"

"I'm glad of that, ma'am," interrupted the stranger, "for I'm expecting my friend, your sheriff, to join me here. A convenient meeting-place, you might say."

"Aye—to be sure," Susan said with perfect calm. "Here's Jeff now." She walked forward to greet the weedy, apologetic little sheriff, who came sidling in, torn between the necessity of upholding the law and embarrassment at affronting the Honeywoods. "Nat," Susan went on smoothly, "you 'n' Johnnie take care of the sheriff and Mr.—"

"Clarkson, Harry Clarkson," supplied the stranger.

"And Mr. Clarkson; see they get acquainted 'n have some punch. I'll fetch some more spices from the kitchen."

"Wouldn't dream of troublin you, ma'am," said Mr. Clarkson, "unless I went with you and helped you. Down South we don't let our ladies lift a finger, 'deed we don't. Besides, I don't like my punch too spicy." He stood squarely in front of Susan. The sheriff gave an embarrassed cough and moved away.

The situation was now quite clear. The slave-catcher had no intention of letting Susan out of his sight. During the course of his work he had become a shrewd judge of character, had often encountered her type during his raids on "Underground" stations, forceful, steely-eyed women fanatical in their determination to meddle with other people's property. She'd be the ring-leader, all right. But he had to go slow, no evidence that this was a station, nothing but a rumour that had reached him in Lynn after his disappointment last night. He'd been sure the nigger wench and her brat were heading to Lynn, but he hadn't been able to find them there. It had been good luck at last to meet up with this young Cubby on the wharves. He'd been quite friendly and helpful, though with that snarl on his face you couldn't tell what he was thinking. Anyway, he'd led the way here.

The slave-catcher's sharp, suspicious eyes darted over the faces while he accepted a glass of punch. Lots of rough fishermen jabbering away in that crazy brogue most of 'em talked; some old women, and a handful of gawky country girls. It was then that he discovered Charity, who had withdrawn to the far corner of the taproom to giggle with Willy Bowen until the music started again and she could make Johnnie dance with her.

She decided that Johnnie had lost interest in Hesper, since he was lounging glumly near the parlour door, and Hesper was standing in back of her Ma 'near the interesting-looking stranger. As a matter of fact, the stranger was staring in her direction, and Charity arched her neck and gave him a sidelong glance. The slave-catcher's eyes gleamed. He sauntered across the room, not neglecting to keep Mrs. Honeywood in sight with the corner of one eye. But this gave Susan a needed opportunity. "Hes," she whispered urgently under cover of stirring the punch, "he's not watchin' you. Go to the kitchen and wait for 'em. You know what to do. I'll keep him in here. Hurry, slip out while he's talking to Charity."

"Oh, Ma—I can't." Leave the fun and dancing, leave Johnnie to Charity's wiles, just when things were going so well. And for what? Some old niggers who probably wouldn't come and in whom she didn't actually believe. This wasn't an adventure at all, it was unpleasant and stupid, and she heartily agreed with her father. Except that the whole thing seemed unreal, everyone playing a part like Bible charades. The slave-catcher and his pistol didn't seem any more convincing than Old Pharaoh and his spear when Willie Bowen had played it. "You'll go *now*," whispered Susan savagely. "I knew you wasn't fit to be trusted." If they'd been alone she would have slapped the girl, shilly-shallying like her father, no grit.

Just then Johnnie turned in the doorway where he had been quietly watching both rooms, Nat in the parlour and the slave- catcher in the taproom. Johnnie saw Hesper's unhappy face beyond her mother's flushed and angry one, and he caught something of the situation. He smiled at Hesper, a smile of warm encouragement, and his lips formed the words "Good luck !" Then he turned his back again.

So that was different. Johnnie expected her to go. Hesper backed quickly and noiselessly towards the wall behind her, where a door led to the buttery passage. Ambrose the fiddler had sat silent in his box since he had stopped playing, his fiddle resting on his knee, his dark face expressionless, staring vaguely up at the beams. Yet at the moment when Hesper opened the buttery door and slipped through he lifted his fiddle and brought the bow across it in a crescendo crash tearing into "Pop Goes the Weasel." So that nobody noticed Hesper's departure.

Hesper went along the passage into the kitchen. It was chilly in here, the little cook-stove nearly out, and no fire in the great hearth. She lit a candle and put some more wood in the stove, and wished she might light the logs that "Looney" had piled in readiness on the big andirons. But Susan certainly would not hold with wasting fuel, when here it was almost May, and, anyway, if those niggers really showed up, and she had no idea how or when, it would be wise not to have too much light in here. She sat down in Gran's old Boston rocker and watched the shadows flicker over the bright pewter on the oak dresser. The sounds of music and dancing came to her faintly, muted by the thick doors and the huge mass of the central chimney. Clearer than the music she heard the intermittent rattle of the shutter from the Borning Room that meant some wind from the north-west. The iron spigot dripped plink-plunk into the stone sink, and the banjo clock gave forth its un-hurried tick. She turned her head and watched the brass pendulum as it swung behind its glass window. It was past nine. They're not coming, she thought, relieved. I won't have to stay much longer. She continued to stare at the clock, tracing in the gloom the familiar painted pictures, a white and gold barkentine sailing on a translucent green sea, and above, on the lyre-shaped neck, a panel of stars and roses. The clock had come into the family with Mary Ellis, Roger's mother, who had not survived his birth. I wonder what makes women die when babies are born, what happens exactly, thought Hesper, trying to lighten the boredom of exile by forbidding speculation, and it was some seconds before her mind registered a new impression. There was a cat miaowing outside the back door.

Must be the Picketts' Tom, she thought, mildly curious, but he wouldn't be apt to come here if he was hungry. Susan disliked and discouraged cats. The miaowing continued faint and insistent, and suddenly she jumped from the rocker, listening. Cat ! "Cat" was the password, but she had applied it only to Cat Island. Her heart beat against her ribs, she picked up the candle and opened the back door. There was nothing to be seen in the darkness but the barn wall and the shadow of the nearest apple tree. And there was silence. She strained her eyes but nothing moved. "Is someone there?" she whispered. No answer. Then she realized she should give the password, if indeed there was any truth in all this. "I thought I heard a cat," she quavered into the darkness, feeling both nervous and foolish.

At once two cloaked and hooded shapes glided round the corner of the house from behind the lilac bush. She held the door silently and they went past her into the kitchen.

The taller shape bent close to her, peering from under the concealing hood, and she saw that it was an old bearded man, a white man. "Is it safe?" he whispered. She shook her head. "Then hide 'em quickly!"

Hesper turned to the other figure, and with that glimpse beneath the hood her daze shattered. The haggard golden-brown face was up-turned in terrified appeal, the liquid black eyes held fear so naked and defiant that Hesper gasped. And against the coloured girl's breast above the shrouding cloak lay a baby's head.

Lord this is real—the thought flashed through her like a galvanic shock; she pushed the woman and the baby towards the broom closet. There were real people in terrible danger. Her trembling fingers released the pin, she slid the door back and gave the girl a candle. "Up the steps," she whispered, "there's food. Don't let the baby cry. The slave-catcher's here."

The coloured girl gave a stifled moan, then noiseless as smoke she vanished up the narrow stairway. Hesper slid the panel, dropped the pin, and shoved the brooms and musket back in place.

The old man stood in the dark, silent until she lit another candle, then he stepped forward, and his steady wise eyes ran over her. "They safe?"

"I think so; nobody knows the hidy-hole but—"

"You're not in this alone?" he interrupted anxiously. "The brig's waiting off the island, the *Scotia* from Halifax. Someone's got to get 'em out there."

"I know, we've arranged, Ma and a fisherman. . . ."

He nodded quickly. "Then I'll be off; left the wagon outside of town in a covert. Should've got 'em off at Lynn, but the chase was too hot. So we had to use you people. Poor things." He shook his white head, looking towards the broom closet. "She's the most pitiful of all those I've helped. God'll help you to help them, too. The cause is just."

He gave her a smile of great sweetness and dignity and wrapped his cloak around him. The door from the taproom was thrown open with a bang. Hesper jumped and her mouth went dry. The slave-catcher walked into the kitchen.

"Pardon me, miss," he said, not looking at Hesper, but at the old man who stood motionless by the settle. "All of a sudden I had a fancy for a drink of water."

I mustn't show anything, I mustn't; she clenched her hands on the folds of her skirt. "Well, take it then," she said tartly, in her mother's voice. "There's the sink and a cup."

Clarkson did not move. "You've a caller, it seems—"

Before she need answer the old man shuffled forward and spoke in a feeble whine. "I seed t' young lass through t' winder, she's a-pokin' up t' stove, so I knocks 'n axes her fur a hundout. No har-rm in that—mister. Me pore ol' belly's empty as a cask." He seemed to have shrunk to half his size, his shoulders hunched, and there was a foolish, vacant look on his wrinkled face.

Gratefully accepting her cue, Hesper hurried to the stove and felt the coffee-pot, which always stood there in readiness.

Clarkson stood his ground, staring at the old man. His sharp lower teeth gnawed on his moustache, his fingers through a gap in his buttoned coat twitched on the handle of his pistol. Suddenly he swung out a long arm and grabbed the old man's shoulder, yanking him into the full light of the candle. "God damn it, you old son-of-a-bitch, I'm sure I've seen you before. In Medford, that's where. You've got a farm with a mighty convenient haycock in it; keep it filled with black-birds, don't you!"

Hesper's cold hands grew clammier. She clattered the poker against the stove lid.

"Lemme be, mister," quavered the old man. "I ain't done nothin' but ax for some vittles. I ain't got no farm no place. I ain't got nothin'."

The fiddle in the taproom blared louder for a moment, and then the noise was shut off, as Susan came into the kitchen and closed the door.

She paused for a second, taking in the scene. The slave-catcher bent menacingly over a trembling old tramp, and Hesper white as the plaster wall, prying at the stove lid with the wrong end of the poker.

"What're you doin' in my kitchen!" She brought her fat freckled hand down sharply across Clarkson's arm, which dropped involuntarily from the old man's shoulder. "Quit bullying this pore old man."

"So you know who he is!" cried Clarkson, turning on her.

"Never saw him afore in my life," answered Susan coolly.

"I say you did! I say you knew he was coming, and you know what he's brought. I'm going to search this house." Clarkson jerked out his revolver, beside himself with fury. His arm tingled from the blow this woman had given it, her cool contempt enraged him. He wasn't a fool, these people couldn't diddle him.

"Sheriff!" he shouted at the top of his lungs, "sheriff, come here!" But Ambrose was playing as hard as he could, and singing too, and many of the dancers sang with him—"As I was walking down the lane, down the lane, down the lane."

"God damn that caterwauling nigger," said Clarkson through his teeth. He looked at the three in the kitchen with him, and he dared not leave them. He cocked the pistol with his thumb, deliberated a moment, then shot through the west outside wall of the room. The old plaster starred and cracked a little around the black hole, the bullet buried itself in a stout oak upright beneath the clapboarding.

That brought them. The fiddle stopped. The sheriff ran in, looking scared, and with him Johnnie, Nat Cubby, and as many of the guests as could squeeze through the entry. And it brought Roger, too. He rushed out of his study to see his kitchen crowded with people and a sleasy black-moustached fellow in the middle of them holding a smoking pistol.

"*What* is this rumpus?" shouted Roger. "What's the meaning of that shot?" His eyes were no longer vague, but bright with anger. He looked at the bullet hole and his marred wall. "I'll have you arrested!"

"Who's this man?" Clarkson growled to the sheriff. The others crowded around open-mouthed.

"Why, that's Mr. Honeywood. Ye didn't oughta go shootin'," answered the sheriff unhappily.

"Oh, you're MISTER Honeywood, so I reckon you know all about it; but I'd be glad to clear your mind, anyhow. I represent the law and I represent Mr. Delacort, owner of the Albermarle Plantation on the Santee River in South Carolina. One of his best nigger wenches lit out with her brat four weeks ago, and he's commissioned me to find her. She's a good breeder and smart, too; worth two thousand dollars. I've reason to believe she's hidden in your house."

"Indeed, she is not!" said Roger, quivering, but in a quieter tone. "You may take my word for it." He glanced at Susan's blank face. How glad she must be now that he had forbidden her to receive the fugitives.

Clarkson was a trifle nonplussed. This one spoke more like a gentleman than the rest of these oafs, and his voice had the ring of truth. Still, the women might be trying something on their own.

"I'm going to search the house and grounds," he said doggedly. He turned his back on the Honeywood family and the old man, to confront the silent group of fishermen. A dozen pairs of eyes stared back at him, expressionless, unwinking. "Any of you men lend me a hand?" he asked. "Can't *all* be god-damn traitorous abolishers."

Cap'n Lane gave an angry grunt, and his fists clenched, otherwise nobody moved.

"You?" said Clarkson at random, pointing at Johnnie with his pistol.

"Why no," said Johnnie softly. "I'd rather not."

Clarkson scowled and pointed to Nat. "You then, you were eager enough to bring me here."

Hesper held her breath, and it seemed to her that the others did, too. Nat stood beside Johnnie, staring at the slave-catcher. He shifted his feet a trifle. His eyes were speculative. "What's there in it for me?" he asked calmly.

"A hundred dollars if we find 'em."

Johnnie swung round, looking down at his friend. "Dirty money, Nat. I never thought it of you. I'm sure your Ma'd not think it of you, either."

A strange expression flickered across the sardonic face. Nat twisted his head and met Johnnie's eyes. "You're a soft fool," he said very low. But he turned on his heel, shoved his way amongst the watching men, and strode through the outside door, slamming it behind him. The little bell jangled and faded to stillness.

"All right, all right," said the slave-catcher. "I'll do it alone. Sheriff, you keep 'em in the taproom. You know your duty?"

The sheriff nodded and coughed, staring at the floor.

"Well, get moving! And if there's any hanky-panky, I'll set the Federals on you, after I've done with you myself."

The sheriff sullenly motioned with his hand, and the fishermen moved back into the taproom to be met by excited or frightened questions from those who hadn't been able to understand what was happening.

"This is an outrage!" cried Roger, while Clarkson himself saw to the bolting of the doors. "You've not the slightest shadow of excuse. I told you there's nobody hidden here."

The slave-catcher twisted his pistol and paid no attention. Susan sat down on her regular stool behind the counter. Her face was white as Hesper's, and the freckles stood out between beads of sweat. The old man in the cloak huddled himself into a dark corner between the fireplace and a keg of beer. Ambrose still sat on his box, staring again at the beams, his fiddle quiet as Clarkson had ordered. Even Charity was subdued and had squeezed herself on a bench beside her mother.

"You—girl," said Clarkson, suddenly pointing at Hesper. "You're coming with me. You can hold the candle, and you know the house."

Hesper glanced involuntarily at her mother; Susan gave a helpless shrug. Helpless, and she looked frightened. Ma! Ma couldn't do anything, and she didn't rightly know what had happened in the kitchen before she came in. Hesper felt an incredulous surge of pity, and then a headier intoxication. Her heart stopped pounding, warmth returned to her hands. She picked up a candlestick, and walked towards the slave-catcher.

"Come then," she said, cool and easy. "And you might stop waving that pistol about—you're not like to use it."

Clarkson looked startled, and she heard Johnnie's laugh. "Good for you, Hessie!"

"We'll start with the outhouses," commanded Clarkson, shoving Hesper ahead of him. She gave him a level, freezing look, and he muttered something that might have been apologetic. He thrust the pistol back into his belt. They went through the kitchen door, having picked up a lantern from its shelf in the entry. Clarkson searched every inch of the barn and the hayloft, thrusting a pitch-fork again and again through the scant heaps of straw, and disturbing only poor "Looney," who was asleep on a mat in a corner. He looked in the pigsty and even in the privy, then returned to the house. He hadn't expected anything of the barn, anyway. Much too obvious for experienced agents like that old son-of-a-bitch greybeard, if he was the man from Medford. Not quite sure. Not sure of anything except that two thousand dollars' worth of merchandise was secreted somewhere along this infernal hostile coast.

He hustled Hesper back to the kitchen, where she stood in the middle of the floor holding the candle while he opened cupboard doors, peered into the Dutch oven and the bottom of the china closet. Once he tapped the plaster wall on the north side between the kitchen and the lean-to, but the sound was dense and flat.

Then he opened the broom closet, and motioned her nearer with the light. Hesper's courage ebbed and her palms grew wet, but he scarcely glanced at the broom and mop and musket in the shallow closet, and had he bothered to sound the false back, he would not have been enlightened. Lot Honeywood and his brother-in-law the pirate had built cannily. The oaken slab was nearly two inches thick and would give out no resonance.

Hesper went from room to room as he ordered her. They entered her father's little study; she saw that when he had been interrupted by the shot, he had been working on the "Memorabilia," and while she held the light for Clarkson, she read one line:

"In olden times in Marblehead, there was many a deed of valour . . ."

The thought did not come clear to her, but as she led the slave-catcher from the buttery, through the larder and into the Borning Room, pausing in each for him to poke and pry and open cupboards, she was puzzled by a question. Why did the olden times seem so romantic— while the present never did? She had a vague realization that this night's work would also seem romantic some day; but it didn't now. That's because I don't know the ending, she thought. Things you hear of from the past, you know what's happened, you don't have to worry. Yet at the moment she wasn't worried. She felt contempt, mastery, inner excitement, not worry, as she led the slave-catcher through the rambling house, even pointing out cupboards and crannies he might overlook. They descended to the cellars; the shallow crude excavation under the old part, the capacious dry rooms under Moses' wing. Clarkson picked up a long stick that was used for stirring the brine in the salt-pork barrel and thrust it into the potato bin and the apple bin. He moved the spare casks of rum and the kegs of beer. He kept a sharp eye for any suspicious markings on the masonry.

The cellars and attics of these old houses were prime choice for hiding-places. He found nothing. He kept a sharp eye on Hesper, too, for any sign of tension, but he could see none. Queer sort of a girl with all that tumbling red hair, her squarish white face set in an expression of chill indifference. Younger than he'd first thought, too; not more than sixteen, and innocent looking for all her loftiness. His certainty that Delacort's fugitive nigger wench was hidden in the house began to weaken; but he pursued the search.

Hesper led him up the newer cellar stairs to the parlour, still brilliantly lit. From the other side of the door they could hear the uneasy shufflings and murmurs of the company imprisoned in the taproom. They continued to the second floor up the beautiful mahogany front staircase. She waited for him to look under the canopied beds and into panelled cupboards in the four spacious bedrooms built by Moses. They descended two steps to the back passage and the old wing. Here there were three bedrooms—her own, her parents' and a spare room; all small and low-ceilinged, sparsely furnished with the rough pine bedsteads and rush-seated slat-back chairs they had always contained.

Clarkson shook his head and snapped. "Now the attic—if that's all down here. House's a regular rabbit warren—up and down, little rooms, big rooms, crazy way to build."

Hesper said nothing, but she saw that the slave-catcher was losing hope, and her spirits rose higher.

There was a bad moment in the attic. Clarkson stumbled around amongst the accumulated lumber of centuries—the spinning wheels and flax-carders, the long cradle and the wooden chests and brass-studded cowhide trunks. Hesper held the candle for him as he demanded it, and he half-heartedly opened a few lids, shook those trunks and chests which were locked. He groped around the masses of the huge central chimneys, the old one of stone, the newer one of brick. He took the candle himself to examine the roof and the rough-hewn rafters, and did not discover so much as a cobweb, so thorough was Susan's house-keeping. "I'll take an oath there's nothing here," he muttered, when a strange little sound came to them, a small choked wail.

"What's that?" cried Clarkson sharply. His hand flew to his pistol, he swung the candle this way and that, peering. The sound had seemed to come from the floor near the old chimney.

It's the baby, thought Hesper, petrified. Pray God it doesn't do it again.

"I didn't hear anything," she said. "For the land's sake, aren't you through up here yet?"

"Shut up! I hear something. Keep quiet."

They stood in the old attic, listening. There was no further sound. Hesper saw plain what must be going on down there, the terrified mother crouching on the pallet in the little cubicle beneath the floor muffling the baby's mouth with her hand or her breast.

"Very likely you heard a rat or the wind in the chimney," said Hesper in just the right tone of boredom and impatience. Strange how easy it was to lie. Stranger yet that these lies were allowed. Ma herself, who was so strict, had been telling them all evening.

As though the slave-catcher had caught an inkling of her thought, he suddenly held the candle to her face. "Look, honey," he said quite gently, "you people don't act like you realized I'm only doing my duty and my job, and the law's solid behind me, remember that. You seem like a smart, nice girl. I'm going to put it to you fair and square." His moustache lifted in an ingratiating smile, the hand that held the candle touched and pressed against her shoulder. "Have you seen, or do you know of, any fugitive slave hidden anywhere on these premises?"

"No," said Hesper, moving her shoulder away. Clarkson made a disgusted sound through his nose. He turned and stamped down the attic stairs in glum silence. Maybe the wench was telling the truth; maybe the whole business was a mare's-nest, after all. Thing to do now was let the old grey-beard loose and follow him. See what he did, come back here later, when they were off guard, maybe find a clue then.

He unlocked the taproom door. "You can all go now," he said sulkily, entering. He had put the pistol back in its holster, and he didn't look at anyone, not even Charity, who thought him most attractive and had spent this imprisoned hour envying Hesper her opportunities, rambling alone all over a dark house with a handsome, sophisticated man like that. What if he was a slave-catcher! Who cared about the silly slaves, anyway. Ma'd often said they were far better off on the plantations than they'd be anywhere else. Now that Mr. Clarkson had satisfied himself he wasn't going to find whatever he'd been looking for, maybe he'd relax and enjoy the party, come and sit by her again, repeat that she was the prettiest little piece he'd laid eyes on in many a long day.

Charity's hopes were dashed. Mr. Honeywood, who always seemed so meek and spineless, suddenly pulled himself up until his head grazed the beams, and stiff as a flag-pole, pointed a long bony finger towards the door. "Your behaviour has been outrageous, sir," he said in a high quivering voice. "Get out of my house."

And Mr. Clarkson, picking up his wide-brimmed black hat from a chair where he had put it earlier, went without a word. The minute he left all the others started leaving, too. Charity sighed. First to last, the party'd been a failure. She'd only danced two dances, there hadn't been any forfeits, and Johnnie Peach hadn't been near her at all.

The sheriff left next, murmuring a sheepish apology. The others followed quickly. No one mentioned the evening's interruption.

"Oi misloike leavin', ma'am," said Cap'n Lane, shaking first Susan's hand and then Roger's; "but Oi needn't tell ye, a seaman keeps ear-rly hours. We've to be abar-rd by cockcrow. Thanks for the good cheer-r."

His wife, Cap'n Caswell, the other couples, the girls and the young fishermen all made similar farewells and filed out.

The Honeywood family was left with Johnnie Peach and the old man, who seemed to be asleep by the fire.

"Disgusting occurrence," said Roger querulously. "Put a hole right through the kitchen wall. Molesting innocent people. I'd like to have the law on him. That's what comes of ever having gotten mixed up with—' He checked himself, remembering that he was not alone with his wife. He scooped a mugful of punch from the depleted bowl and swallowed it irritably. "What's to be done with that old tramp?" he said, pointing.

Susan had started piling used mugs on a tray and crumbing the table. There were mounds of gingerbread, brandy-snaps and saffron tarts still untouched.

"Never mind him, Roger," she answered quietly. "I'll care for him. You go to bed. Hes and Johnnie'll help me clear up."

Roger grunted. "Well, good night, all. If that bostard comes back, don't let him in." And his use of the universal Marblehead epithet marked the extent of his perturbation. He stalked out.

Susan put down the tray of mugs; she and Johnnie both looked at Hesper. "What happened, Hes? Tell us quick from the beginning."

Hesper complied, speaking in short nervous whispers, while Johnnie and her mother listened anxiously.

"Now what's to be done?" said Susan, shaking her head. "How'll we get 'em out o' here."

The old man raised his head, pushing off his hood. "Where's the fiddler?" he said.

Susan jumped. "I'd clean forgot you, sir. The fiddler bolted the minute Clarkson opened the door; he looked pretty skeered."

The old man nodded. "Too bad. He knew something of what was up. But he'll be no use now. You got your boat ready?" he asked Johnnie.

"Aye. She's pulled behind a rock, windward side o' Gerry's Island; nobody'd see her there tonight. I calc'lated we could sneak 'em down through the Honeywood lot, and across Little Harbour to the island near dry-shod before the water rises much. Row 'em over to Cat from there."

"Good. But can you manage alone?"

" 'Twill be hard. Tide and wind's both against."

"I'd help you—though I've a feeble back and no knowledge of the water, except that I'm worse needed for decoy." His bearded lips lifted. "I know our friend the slave-catcher's mind better than he knows it himself. Having drawn a blank here, he's lurking outside to follow me. I'll lead him a good chase, make it interesting enough to keep him with me. It'll give you time." He stood up and went to the table, crammed a tart into his mouth, and a handful of gingerbread into his pocket. "By your leave, ma'am."

"O' course—take all—you've got spunk, sir. I hope we've as much. We'll do our best. But after this the U.G. mustn't use us. Roger's dead agin it. I had to diddle him tonight."

"Yes, I saw." He smiled his singularly sweet and warming smile. "Anyway, we're building up the overland line, westward to the border. I must hurry; but who's to help you row, young man?" he added, frowning.

"I am," said Hesper firmly. "I'd thought of it earlier."

Johnnie's worried face cleared. "Gorm—I guess you could at that, Hes. You used to be right handy for a girl."

Susan opened her mouth and shut it again. It was the only solution now, but her heart misgave her. There was always danger on the sea— who to know better than she who had lost sons, and her father, too. If anything should happen to Hes, and Roger not knowing either. Still, what was right was right, and risks must be taken.

"You sure o' the brig, sir?" she said, rolling up the brandy-snaps in a napkin and handing them to the old man.

He nodded. "Cap'n Nelson never fails. He's heart and soul for the cause, and well paid, too. Good luck. God'll rejoice in you for this night's work. I daren't shake hands, for I believe our bloodhound's lurking by that window. Give us twenty minutes, then move quickly." He wrapped himself in his cloak and shuffled across the floor and out the taproom door.

"Hes," said Susan briskly, handing Hesper a diluted mug of punch. "Drink this."

Hesper obeyed, startled. Ma'd never let her touch anything stronger than dandelion wine. It tasted awful; for a second she thought she must retch, then a pleasing tingle of warmth glowed in her stomach.

"Change your clothes—I'll give you Willy's oilskins. Johnnie, keep watch outside, be sure he's gone." Susan bustled her daughter upstairs. As soon as Hesper had taken off the blue poplin, her mother reappeared with a flannel shirt and complete set of oilskins. She kept her drowned sons' clothes in a locked sea-chest in her bedroom, though the fact was never mentioned.

"Good thing you're tall," she said grimly. She pulled down the braid of red hair and tucked it inside the stiff yellow jacket, jammed on the stiffer black-brimmed sou'wester and fastened it under Hesper's chin. "Anybody at ten paces 'd take you for a fisher boy." And suddenly she leaned near and kissed Hesper on the cheek, an occurrence so unprecedented that they both were flooded with embarrassment.

"Well, are your feet glued to the floor?" snapped Susan. "Get moving —hurry."

They found Johnnie pacing up and down the kitchen, also attired in his oilskins. "Gorm." He stared at Hesper. "I'd never've known ye." He chuckled and gave her shoulder a resounding thwack. "M'hearty young fisherman!" But catching Susan's minatory eye he went on quickly, "They've gone all right. Old man stumpin' along up Circle Street an' the slave-catcher creepin' through the shadows a few rods behind. Wind's slackenin' some—praise be—but tide's comin' in fast."

Susan pulled the window curtains tighter and opened the closet door. "Call 'em, Hes!" The girl manipulated the panel and ascended the narrow steps, her creaking clumsy oilskins catching against the chimney's rough stone. "Come down," she called gently into the darkness. "It's safe now."

There was a soft movement in the hidy-hole, and Hesper backed down the steps. The mulatto girl followed at once. She stood, crouching over the baby and trembling. Her black eyes slid from one to the other of them, her golden brown face was a mask of fear.

"Here now," said Susan, "stop shaking. You're almost free. These two'll get you to the ship." She doused the candle and opened the back door.

Johnnie went first, then the slave girl, then Hesper. The moonless night was overcast with heavy, dark clouds, yet was not too dark for Hesper's and Johnnie's keen young eyes. They followed the familiar path between the vegetable and herb patches, past the apple trees and around the great elm tree that marked the eastern boundary of the Honeywood lot. They crept in the shadow of Pitman's fish warehouse, and Johnnie paused to inspect the cove. All the fish-flakes had been covered with tarpaulin for the night, all dories beached and made fast. Their peering eyes could discern no movement in the darkness. There was no noise but the lap and suck of the water on the shingle, and then the crunch of their heavy fishing-boots as Johnnie led the way over the shore pebbles to the strip of land which at low tide connected the mainland and Gerry's Island. The slave girl glided silent as a forest doe between them. As they reached the island the rising waters met and wet her feet and she gasped from the sudden cold, but made no other sound.

They crossed the bare little island to the ocean side, where Johnnie had hidden his new green dory between two sheltering rocks. Johnnie tugged until it floated, then guided the two girls while they clambered in. He placed the slave-girl in the stern, and as she settled herself the baby woke up and gave a fretful cry. She crouched lower over it, a dark shape against the darker rocks behind, and they heard her crooning, "Hush—hush—hush." Johnnie put Hesper on the forward thwart and himself amidships. He fitted in the oars. "All set, Hes," he whispered. "Pull slow and steady. Don't get winded and don't get skeered."

" 'Course not," she answered scornfully, for they were still in the lee of Peach's Point and the rowing easy. She had never rowed this mile and a half stretch to Cat Island before, but she had sailed it several times. Of late years, since the Salem Steamboat Co. had bought the island and built there a large summer hotel, it had been rechristened Lowell's Island, and become a favourite sailing goal for Marblehead children, who amused themselves gaping at the fashionably dressed excursionists the steamer deposited at the wharf. In the last century the island had still another name—Hospital Island, from the smallpox pest-house situated upon it; but Marbleheaders, ever indifferent to ephemeral fancies, continued to call it by its original name. Hesper and Johnnie rowed steadily towards the east, and the four heavy eight-foot oars dipped together in a smooth rotating rhythm, until gradually they drew abreast of the lighthouse on the point of the Neck to the south.

This was easy, thought Hesper, not near as bad as Johnnie seemed to think. But in another moment they reached the open channel, and the brisk north wind hit them full force. The waves, at first merely choppy, grew bigger until their tumbling white crests slid by at eye-level in the darkness. The staunch little dory shuddered and twisted and climbed, and slipped down again into the troughs. Hesper lost her stroke, and found that over and over she was beating her oars on empty air. Spray showered on her back and ran down the oilskins.

The slave-girl began to cry softly, "Oh lawdy, lawdy, save us," and they heard her retching.

"Steady on, Hes!" cried Johnnie, twisting his head. "Ship your starboard oar, bear all you've got to port, we're bein' blown off course."

She obeyed, pulling now with both hands at the port oar, trying to time it with Johnnie's powerful strokes. The dory swung slowly back into the wind. Sweat poured down her face and neck and between her breasts; her arms and shoulders began to ache with a fiery pain. The greyish white-tipped masses rocked beneath them, the bilges sloshed with deepening water.

Hesper clenched her teeth and pulled, watching the lighthouse creep inch by inch astern. She heard Johnnie's unconscious grunts as he exerted all his strength on each down pull. I can't go on, she thought once as her oar twisted and buried itself in a mountain of water. Her hands were raw inside the leather fishing mittens, a knife was twisting in her shoulder-blades. But she clung to the oar, yanked it out and went on. Forward—pull—back. Forward—pull—back. Mechanical and mindless. There was no room for fear, nor pity for the poor drenched